Leigh Anne,

"No amount of dirt
can cover up every
ember."

Best,
Akira Hersh

For my teacher,
who had the courage to love me
and the wisdom to show me how
to love myself.

❧

Acknowledgments

To my family: You are the colors, the sounds, and the textures that illuminate, harmonize, and soften my life. Thank you.

To my editor, John Knight: You brought clarity and simplicity in just the right places. Thank you for your insight.

To my Cover and Interior Designer, Xavier Comas: You are a master artist. Thank you for seeing the symbols and themes in my story and giving them a beautiful visual expression.

To The Wine Spot, Appletree Books, and Loganberry Books in Cleveland, Ohio: Thank you for letting me sit in your lovely spaces and write.

He who learns must suffer.
And even in our sleep, pain
that cannot forget falls drop by drop
upon the heart, and in our own despair,
against our will, comes wisdom
to us by the awful grace of God.

AESCHYLUS

Boy In The Hole

by Akiva Hersh

CHAPTER I

Big Balls

"Well, those are the biggest balls I've ever seen on a baby," cried Audrey, her crooked fingers swiping, dabbing at Jacob as though shelling peas. "I'm gonna get you clean. Yes, I am. Gonna get you all clean from that poopie diaper you made." Audrey stuck her fingers under the stream of water, then turned off the faucet. Not too hot; don't want to scald him, she thought. Hot water is for dirty things like the wash, showers, enemas. "You're so precious, I could just eat you up," Audrey said.

Was it normal, Rose asked herself, watching over Audrey's shoulder, for a grandmother to talk that way? Was it normal for a grandmother to comment on the size of her grandson's testicles? Were Jacob's testicles normal? In case something was wrong, perhaps a swelling, or a reddening she hadn't noticed, Dr. Wilkinson should take a look. She would call him tomorrow. For her mother always made her feel—as she searched anything new with such scrutiny, pointing out this flaw or that in an urgent tone, suggesting one had made a mistake or caused her embarrassment—always made her feel inadequate, lacking, unworthy.

When did Mama's hands get so old? wondered Rose, watching Audrey rubbing the baby oil into Jacob's skin. She used to be able to count the brown liver spots on her mother's hands, youth now fading, her black hair swathing with white streaks as though a painter had trailed several thin brushes down a black canvas.

The way Audrey looked at Jacob bothered Rose—it was a look as if nothing else in the world mattered. Her gaping smile and wide-spaced teeth revealed silver caps flashing like mesh in a flour sifter. "I'm gonna eat you, you're just so sweet." Rose imagined her mother lifting one of Jacob's fingers to her mouth and biting off an end.

"Mama let me finish."

"These cloth diapers ain't easy to get on. Let me show you first."

That brutal force of motherhood, withheld from her daughter, silently waited beneath years and was now waking and warming to Jacob. Audrey had refused to hold Rose the first day and night she brought her home from the hospital (Audrey's sister, Thelma, had told Rose the story) and though Audrey had denied it, and claimed Thelma was confused, she admitted she didn't need another child after Donald. The family didn't need a girl. Wasn't a good idea for Klaus to have a girl around, as Audrey found out on her honeymoon.

BOY IN THE HOLE

Audrey met Klaus Ramburg working at the Florida Citrus canning plant outside Lakesville in 1941. Two years later they stood at the altar of the First Baptist Church in Holly Berry, Florida before God, smiling, vowing to be faithful, promising to stay together in health and in sickness. But neither pledged to shield the other from the vilest parts of themselves nor to protect the ones they loved from the monsters they harbored. Their pact was meant to keep secrets; to deny, and to minimize the other's sins.

The evening of their wedding, after the reception, Klaus and Audrey arrived at The Lakesville Terrace Hotel. It was a grand hotel with deluxe suites suitable for special occasions and simple rooms, such as the one Klaus reserved—a single full bed and a bathroom would do.

A valet parked their car, and into the lobby they walked, giddy, hand in hand, heads held high. The porter brought the couple to their room overlooking a lake. Audrey inspected the room while Klaus tipped the boy. Not a flap of wallpaper was unglued. The carpet was bright and clean. She found a little dust on the dresser missed by the cleaner. If she tried, she could pick up a whiff of mold in the yellow-green afternoon air.

She started for the bathroom to freshen up. Klaus closed the door to the room and locked it.

"Lay down on the bed," he instructed.

"I want to go—"

"I said get on the bed." She did.

"Now turn over."

Grinning, she peered over her shoulder as he lifted her dress, exposing her panties.

"What are you going to do?" she asked, like she was

watching him tinker with a car engine.

Curiosity overpowered her fear. For Audrey was from French stock—her people were courageous, dauntless, incredulous. Hadn't they been pioneers? The last word was never surrendered.

"Lie still," he said.

How Klaus loved to titillate. He never wanted to reveal a woman all at once. Under the band of her panties, he slipped his finger, taking his time, watching for her desire in a glance, in a giggle, in a blush. Silk slipped, exposing smooth white skin. She's ready now, Klaus thought, her intimate things flicked from feet to floor.

Only for a moment did Audrey hesitate to display her consent. It was the pain that worried her. Mother had said men needed to have their way, and if you find a good one, everything'll be all right. Maybe he was a good one. Mother said you'll know after he's done. Maybe he'll be really good.

"Look at that picture on the wall," said Klaus. It was a portrait of one of the lakes surrounding the hotel.

"It sure is pretty. The swans are so—"

"I didn't tell you to talk. Just look at that picture and be still."

Audrey concentrated on the swans, a mother and her cygnets floating toward a clump of cattails. Maybe he'll do this to me, and I'll have a baby, too.

She recalled their wedding reception just hours ago, laughing with Beatrice, her Maid of Honor, about how she never thought the day would come she'd leave Mother. She saw herself in her white gown walking among the pink and brown streamers and paper bells, slicing a piece of the tall cake; all of it seemed like a fairy tale, like make-believe. When had she grown up? *Please, Lord, bless me and Klaus with a baby.*

In the small room, among everyday things, the bedside table, the mirror, the vase of white and red carnations, suddenly the bed darkened with his shadow. He straddled her legs; released his belt. The mattress quivered as if in accord with Audrey's anticipation.

It's a firm bed, thought Audrey, not like at Mother's. Not my bed anymore. Wonder what kind of bed he'll get me. It don't need to be so firm like this one.

Klaus pressed her face into the sheets. She screamed as he forced himself into her.

"Klaus, that hurts! Please, honey, you're hurting me."

He put his rough hand over her mouth; thrusting; grunting; slapping. On and on he went, then strained deep inside her until he finished.

Crawling off, he said, "Keep looking at that picture."

Enmity and terror were conceived in that room, and among the crumpled sheets and blood and semen and the swishing of ducks on water splashing, the nosy fly buzzing, darting, swooping, begging to know—"Do you see me?"—the horror was never interrupted nor the air of control as if the inquiry needn't be addressed: you don't matter.

Audrey heard his footsteps.

Crack!

She wanted to look at the source of the sound. She turned her head and felt a hard whack across her back.

"I told you to watch that picture."

She stared at the portrait of the swans, the blue of

13

the lake, which was the blue of robin's eggs. *This is not happening to me.* She looked at the cygnets, feeling pity for them. *I'm that mama swan with her babies. Please, Jesus let me*—she felt pressure against her anus. Klaus teased the knob of the broomstick from one hole to the other.

"Don't take your eyes off that picture."

He couldn't decide where to plunge the broomstick. Either hole would teach her. *Better put it where I ain't been yet.* A swift twist and push. Audrey yelled out as the broomstick went in as far as a finger length. Klaus muffled her sounds with a pillow. During the war, he'd learned how to control squirming young French girls.

"What are you doing here, Audrey? Your honeymoon isn't over for two more days," asked Beatrice.

"I need to show you something. Come to the bathroom."

"Is everything all right?" Beatrice closed the door and turned as Audrey pulled out bloody towels from between her legs.

"Sweet Lord Jesus, what happened to you, honey?"

"He did something real bad, Beatrice."

"Have you seen a doctor?"

"Don't you bring that up or you'll never hear from me again."

"You're setting something up here, Aud, something he's going to come back to over and over."

"Are you going to help me or not?"

"Get undressed. I'll draw an Epsom bath."

White tiles, white tub, white salts dissolving; bright

red drops diffusing into ropy clouds and settling; a thousand things one knew about life utterly vanished.

Audrey pricked her finger on the metal safety pin. She sucked the blood before she tried again to pin the diaper. She cooed at Jacob. Of her two children, Donald pleased most, though he hadn't given her a grandson. He'd given her another girl to worry about. But this baby boy was the best thing Rose ever did in her life, even if the father was a Catholic who led her away from the Baptist church.

And now, seeing Rose there, waiting to hold her little baby, waiting for her husband to come home from the mine, Audrey wondered what he saw in her—she must've lured Edwin Murtaugh sexually. That's how girls like Rose got rich, smart, athletic boys—for she was cold, unkind, a devil. Now Edwin wasn't the same, returned from Vietnam damaged. Rose hadn't counted on that. But infliction one conceals by ambition.

But what had she thought? Edwin would come back a hero, and they would escape to a mansion in Tampa? Miami? Now they lived in a tiny trailer camper on a slab of concrete Daddy poured for them not forty-five feet from the house. Audrey had a keen sense, as she contemplated their future, of disappointment. She couldn't see how Edwin could quit a good job at the mine and go back to college to get some business degree. And how could a man make a woman work to support her own family? People would surely talk. That man—Audrey's resentment rose in her breast—would never succeed.

And for a girl concerned with people's opinions,

15

(since she was old enough to talk), Rose always brought disgrace on the family, especially when it came to boys. Cruising in their cars, parking at the movies, running around with them by herself to do Lord knows what. *It's that bad seed from Klaus.* Now she wants to work and let her man go to school. *It ain't natural.* She must bring it up with Klaus so he could knock some sense into her. Indecent to leave her grandbaby motherless. *Lord Jesus, don't let this baby boy have any bad seed in him.*

"Mama, I've got to go next door to see if Mrs. Crawley can watch Jacob tomorrow morning."

"Now whatever for? You need to be home with that baby. Need to have a routine with him."

"I've got to go pick up my unemployment check. The line starts at 7 a.m."

When one practices the Catholic method, one must plan for any inevitability. Not Rose and Edwin. Rose lost her job after she became pregnant. Her moderate unemployment check would hold them until she could get a job, but no consideration had been given as to who would care for the child. Audrey worked for the county, Klaus the railroad. The only option was for Rose to ask a neighbor to babysit. Dr. Wilkinson told her having a short break from the baby would help with her depression.

But what if Mrs. Crawley left Jacob to cry alone in the crib? Or what if she picked him up and, having grown used to the scent of his mother's breasts, he couldn't stand Mrs. Crawley's odor and turned colicky, what then? Or worse, what if Jacob began to forget her? What if he preferred Mrs. Crawley more?

"Does Edwin know you're plannin' on runnin' off in

the mornin' and leavin' that baby with our neighbor?"

"We don't have a choice, Mama. I gotta have that check."

"Run on then. I'll keep Jacob with me."

"I'm bringing him so I can introduce Mrs. Crawley to him."

"That woman's raised three of her own. You don't need to be taking this baby out in the air. Leave him here with me."

"Yes, ma'am." Rose couldn't argue with her. Couldn't argue and win. She would give Jacob a warm bottle in the morning before she left and maybe he'd sleep until she returned. She'd worry about it later, just like Scarlet O'Hara, God as her witness.

Audrey cuddled with Jacob, rocking away his last hold on the world before sleep. She never cuddled her granddaughter, Carol Alice. Her manner with the girl was entirely different; she was sedated, sterile, hard. A hired professional. She had always favored Donald, too.

She just likes boys better, thought Rose. *Something isn't right. Something isn't normal.* Then dread, like a gale, tore across her mind, splitting this thought from that one, like boat-shaped petals torn from a lily by a scattering wind.

"Now, I'm going to put you down, Jacob. I've got to clean up this filthy house before your Granddaddy gets home."

The house was spotless. But she laid him in his bassinet and turned on the mobile. "Bye, Baby Bunting" played softly over his head. Rose walked out the back door, down the gravel road to go speak to Mrs. Crawley. ❧

CHAPTER II

Have a Raleigh Raleigh Christmas

"Your mother smokes like a chimney. I'm not having her come into my new house and stink it up with cigarette smoke."

"Well, I can't ask her to go stand outside, Rose. It'll be cold," said Edwin.

"Then ask your father for extra money to close in the porch so she can sit in the sunroom." Edwin slid his hand off Roses's thigh and walked across the trailer to the television.

"You're not putting on a game now, Eddie?"

"I want to catch the college score before the golf tournament."

"You don't need to watch every match your brother's in."

It was wrong what happened to Edwin, thought Rose, the government sending him off to war, Tommy dodging the draft because of a dislocated shoulder (which didn't stop him from playing golf); Edwin losing his own chance

19

to be a professional golfer—he would have been better than Tommy—it was wrong Edwin suffering so much hatred from the very country that sent him off to war. But after living next to Mama and Daddy for three years, God had rewarded him by moving them to Pierceville, helping them buy the furniture store, and letting them build a home of their own in Rolling Green. God had decreed life was going to get better, thought Rose.

Soon the house would be finished, and they would move out of the double-wide and out of trailer park, and people would see Rose Murtaugh wasn't trash. They would see she had married a good man. They would see she gave birth to a beautiful boy. Soon they would be able to afford nice things, and the whole country would get better; Carter would beat Ford and turn things around. Maybe people could get gas again. Carter was from Georgia, and Daddy was from Georgia. Good people came from Georgia.

Life would be perfect then, but Rose couldn't bear to think of Christmas without her mother and father. Did it occur to Edwin, she asked herself, her first Christmas without them might be depressing? Did it matter at all how she felt?

And there would be no smoking in the house. She was already put out over Edwin spending their money on liquor to make Highballs for Thomas Sr. and Tom Collins for Elaine. Can't they go without it? Bring their own? Smokers and drinkers, to hell with the whole lot.

"Let's go see the house, Edwin. I need to get out of this trailer. I'm feeling down."

"All right, dear. I'll get Jacob."

The freshly painted Sherman-Williams "Relative White" walls of the hallway leading from the avocado-colored kitchen to the bedrooms were nothing more than vertical racetracks to three-year-old Jacob.

"VROOM," he screamed. His shiny red Formula One Hot Wheels left faint black scratches along the walls.

"I'm fast," he yelled. The smell of "new" was exciting, and Jacob had to run. He had to be a racecar because it was the fastest thing he knew. Up and down the walls he raced; roaring the engine; screeching the brakes; squealing the tires.

Their mobile home down the road at Hidden Ranch trailer park was cramped; it was not a place for a boy to race. Hollering like an Indian, he ran up and down the hallway there on his stick horse.

"No, no, no. Go outside. I have a headache," Rose would scream.

The old people ushered a sharp "Shhh!" as Jacob galloped along the sidewalks near the shuffleboard courts.

Having heard the scraping on her new paint, Rose came upon Jacob harshly.

"Look, Mommy, my racecar!"

"Dammit, Jacob. You're going to ruin Mommy's walls. You should know better." Rose grabbed the little car and threw it on the floor. "Go play somewhere else."

"Son, the car's tires will scratch, and the walls have just been painted," said Edwin, trying to explain. "Go play outside, okay?" Jacob's bottom lip quivered. "You scared him, Rose."

"You're babying him, Edwin. Just like Elaine coddled you."

"Oh, stop it. Just because Mom and Dad didn't spank us kids, but you and Donald got the shit beat out of you doesn't mean Mother babied me. Let's go check out the shag carpet in the Florida room."

Rose set her point aside—for the time being. For having started a cut, Rose was the kind to see it through, clean past the bone. She knew it hadn't occurred to Edwin that his parents felt guilty for breaking his neck in the car wreck when he was five. Had they not been drunks, she figured, they might have been stricter with him and disciplined him through his bouts of mental paralysis. Negligence begets incompetence.

Into the sunken Florida room they stepped. It was larger than a den; a space adequate for a television, bookshelves, a large sofa, chairs, and a service window into the kitchen with a bar and two leather bar stools. Fuzzy carpet, brown, yellow, and orange, spread out like lava reaching the wood-paneled walls, flowing up the single step to the dining room, and stopping cleanly at the lime green carpet with dark green flecks. Ivory drapes and white bamboo furniture gave the formal dining a faux British Colonial feeling.

From the sliding glass door, Rose could see the concrete slab that would become the porch. If Edwin could persuade Tom to pay for it, she'd have a sunroom. Jacob could play safely there year-round, get out of her hair while she watched *Donahue* and her soaps, and Elaine could sit and smoke.

Squatting on the slab of pavement, framed in a spotlight of sun, was Jacob holding a twig between his fingers like a surgeon with a scalpel. He had stabbed a roach. Just before bringing the bug to his mouth, Rose yelled for him to stop.

"Bugs are dirty. Put that down. Now come inside and wash your hands. Don't ever touch those again."

"He's just a little boy, Rose. Boys play with bugs. You're going to make him afraid to get dirty."

"I'd rather him be afraid to get dirty than him get sick. Do you want him to get sick, Eddie?"

"Good God, you're impossible!"

Edwin couldn't help himself; it was hard to respect her; for he came from better stock. His family hailed from New York; Thomas Sr. played for the Dodgers, then was hired as safety manager at Mobil Chemical. His father put her father to shame. Klaus grew up poor and dropped out of school and worked on the railroads.

But that was uncalled-for, thought Rose. Didn't Edwin know better than to fight with her in front of Jacob? He had no idea how to parent. Who had read the books about raising children? She had. Who had read Dr. Benjamin Spock, who said spanking teaches the child the adults have the power? She had. And she knew children respected power. And the Bible said, spare the rod, spoil the child.

Now Dr. Spock never suggested parents should spank their children; in fact, he was against it. And the words, "Spare the rod, spoil the child," are nowhere to be found in the Bible. But this was Rose's unique ability, a trait that helped her survive the Ramburg household. She had the skill to read or hear a piece of information and lift the part that served her and completely change its meaning into something new, while still attributing the quote to the original author. She would employ this new apothegm to spur her on in difficult times, or carry it as a battle cry in a fight with Edwin, or throw it down as a point of fact to crush a friend who attempted to reason with her.

Rose inspected Jacob's hands. "Did you see your new room?"

"Pretty blue carpet," Jacob said. "Can we get a puppy?"

"No, your Maw Maw and Grandaddy would never understand why we have a dog. Besides, I'd be the one to have to take care of it."

"We live on a half-acre lot, Rose. The dog doesn't have to be an indoor dog." Edwin was looking out the window. He didn't notice the lone silver leafless tree shaking pathetically or the brown grass in the side yard. He saw a lawn covered in shamrock green Zoysia grass, a private putting green just off to the left; a playset with a slide and swings; a pool with a wooden deck; a fenced-in section for Jacob's dog.

"Daddy hates dogs. I'd never hear the end of it." Rose dug more dirt from underneath Jacob's fingernails.

Jacob had forgotten the dog. "When are we moving?" Fear flashed across his face.

"The house should be finished soon, son." Edwin patted Jacob's head. "Aren't you excited?"

"What if it's not done?" Jacob knew the plan was to be in the house before Christmas. He knew his Nana and Papa were supposed to make a big visit. He didn't know how all of his toys would get packed and not get lost or broken. He didn't know how the house would be ready in time for his family to move in and look nice for Nana and Papa. But there was something worse than all that.

"What if Santa can't find our new house, Daddy?"

"Don't worry, son. It'll all be okay. He has helpers who will find our address."

"But who will tell the helpers?"

"Mommy and Daddy." Edwin thought about going outside to see where he could plant the azaleas in the spring.

"What if they forget to tell Santa?"

"They won't. Don't worry." A row of boxwood in front of the house, then maybe the azaleas.

"How will all my toys get here?" Jacob was spiraling. Thinking about the toys made him remember his bed, and how Mommy and Daddy had said he would be getting a new one because he'd outgrown his old one. Where would they get it? He had to remember to ask about that. He tugged on Rose's blouse.

"Mommy, what if—"

"Enough, Jacob. Go play."

"Edwin, you've got to talk to your father about getting the extra money for the porch. I'm not going to have her smoke in this house."

"I'll talk to him, Rose. He's been making a big toy box for Jacob for Christmas. I'll tell him a screened-in porch will be the perfect spot for it, and it'll be a nice place for Mother to be warm when she smokes."

Edwin had the gift of the silver tongue, and if he needed, he'd promise to turn the Dead Sea into living waters. Mobil gave him his job back when he returned from Da Nang, but it was a sham. The position paid the same, but he had to drive two hours to work in a mine instead of behind a desk in an air-conditioned office. Rose

25

knew his ego was insulted, and she didn't blame him for how he felt. Edwin wanted to finish his degree in Business Management, but he didn't want to work in the mines for Mobil. Rose wanted an impressive, well-paid husband. Vietnam taught him he wouldn't be bossed around. Rose wanted to travel. Edwin was smart—smarter than the average guy—and that's how he survived the jungle. Rose didn't want to work. Edwin needed to work for himself.

Since Thomas Murtaugh, Sr. helped him land the Mobil job, Edwin would have to assure his father of two things: he would complete his degree, and there would be no fallout from his resignation. Edwin prepared his pitch like a politician on the campaign trail. His father advised him on a few matters and stayed out of his way. Then Edwin painted a picture for Rose she couldn't resist. He would work mornings (part-time) on a nine-hole golf course in Lakesville, then drive to the University of Florida for his afternoon and evening classes. She would draw unemployment for as long as she could, then find work as a secretary. He sold her on the office job too. He told her she'd get a taste of being a "modern woman" and a "chance to meet friends," and he reminded her Dr. Wilkinson thought it was important for her to have a little time away from Jacob to "stave off the depression." The big carrot on the stick was moving away from Lakesville. She never dreamed he would land her in Pierceville, Florida.

"When will Nana and Papa be here?"

"Very soon. Go play until they get here, son."

"Where are they going to sleep, Mommy?"

"I've told you. They're going to sleep in the Florida room, on the pull-out couch."

"But the Christmas tree will be on. What if they can't sleep with all the lights?"

"The lights won't be on."

"How will Santa find our house, Mommy?"

"Get outside and play, Jacob. You're making Mommy so nervous."

Fixing her eyes on Jacob, she cast him her sternest look, a Joan Crawford glare. The Murtaugh's visit had put her at her wit's end. What would they have to talk about when Edwin was at the furniture store, and she had to entertain them? She would be able to keep busy with the constant cleaning that would need to be done, laundry, dusting, dishes. But what if she had to spank Jacob in front of them? Thomas Sr. would not hesitate to give her a piece of his mind about that.

And then there was religion. Would they talk about mass? Would Jacob ask a thousand questions about Mary and Jesus? There was no way she was taking her son to a Catholic mass, even if Jacob wanted to go. Their family would attend Christmas Eve service at First Lutheran Church. This was the compromise she and Edwin had agreed on. Coming from a Baptist background, getting as far as the Lutherans was more than fair, she thought. They don't have the priests and all that incense; they let women sing in the choirs; Edwin could be an elder; Holy Communion isn't quite the body of Jesus; it was a good trade. But she was still going to hell according to Mama and Daddy and Donald. But so were Elaine, Thomas, Thomas Jr., and Edwin's younger brother, Dennis. All

Catholics were going to hell. The Lutherans were a good bet, she thought.

Afraid of his mother, Jacob crouched behind a chair and watched her vacuum the carpet in the Florida room. The sucking pulled at the tinsel on the Christmas tree as she lifted red and green packages to rid the floor of the brown nettles. This he enjoyed very much. When she wasn't watching, he would have to try for himself to see how close he could get the vacuum to the tinsel before it got inhaled, as if the vacuum was a hungry monster and the tinsel a bad guy getting snorted into its whirling, toothy mouth.

"Jacob, clean up your toys in the sunroom so Nana can sit out there in peace."

"But I'm playing."

"If you don't clean up every toy on that porch, I'm going to throw them all away, and you'll get nothing for Christmas."

Jacob dashed past the tinsel-eating monster, opened the sliding glass door, and sat on the specked-black, forest green indoor/outdoor carpet. The afternoon sun filtered through the dark brown tint on the screened porch windows. He looked at the toys scattered across the floor and began to play with a red Tonka fire engine. Would Santa bring him the Weebles playset and the Mr. Potato Head he asked for in his letter? What if he didn't clean the porch, liked Mommy said? Could Mommy send away the gifts Santa brings? He didn't understand how this worked. He was afraid to ask her. Better ask Daddy.

Edwin arrived home from the store. He showered and dressed and waited. His parents still hadn't arrived.

They were to go to Tudor's steakhouse for dinner, Thomas Sr.'s treat.

Rose was relieved she didn't have to cook the first night, although she wouldn't be able to relax at all because she always felt the Murtaughs offered to do kind things with strings attached. Elaine had called a few days ago to tell Rose they wanted to *offer* to take everyone out for dinner the first night they came. They wanted to celebrate the new house, the new store, and give Rose a break from cooking. *Offer* was a suspicious word. Why didn't she just say they wanted to take everyone out? Why *offer*?

Elaine used that word because she hoped Rose would refuse, which Rose did: "But dinner out is so expensive, and I don't mind cooking. Edwin has gotten me such a nice kitchen," which is what she knew Elaine wanted her to say.

"It's no bother, Rose. We want to do it," which is what Elaine knew Rose was expecting to hear.

"I really think Eddie wants us to have meals at home," said Rose.

"You'll be cooking plenty, dear. It's just one night out." Elaine had obeyed her husband's order to invite her daughter-in-law to dinner.

Rose tried to turn it down because she knew Edwin would not want his father to foot the bill because Thomas Jr. always paid when the family got together. He was expected to. Tommy was playing golf on TV, had been invited to Ford's Oval Office, was friends with Bob Hope, Hank Williams, and that negro who plays George Jefferson. But Eddie was just the owner of a little furniture store in Pierceville, Florida. He had to borrow the money from Elaine's sister, Faith, to buy the franchise on condition that when the business was successful enough to bring in a partner, he'd take on her son Paul (who would have to move his family from Long Island).

A ruthless CPA, Faith did not let a month go by without sending a statement reminding Rose and Edwin of their debt and their promise.

The doorbell rang, and Jacob went running. "They're here. They're here."

Edwin let his parents in. Rose came to the door and tried to contain Jacob. "Nana, come look at the screened-in porch. This is where you have to smoke."

Edwin and Rose chuckled, embarrassed by the child and caught off-guard by how much Jacob paid attention. "Now Jacob, your Nana can smoke wherever she wants." Edwin didn't look at Rose but went out to the car with his father to bring in the luggage and gifts.

"The house is beautiful," said Elaine.

"Thank you. We're still fixing everything, but we're very proud of it. It's not a mansion in the Dunes like Tommy's but—"

"Well, you have to live within your means, Rose. And he doesn't live in a mansion. It's a nice house on a prestigious golf course. But that's what he and Linda can afford. What you and Eddie have here is nice for your family, and you need to appreciate it."

"Yes, ma'am," Rose said, like a kicked dog. She knew her place, when to be quiet. That came to her naturally. She learned to anticipate what her parents needed; this one silently stewing about his hard day, his sore feet, the rubbing they needed. The other ranting about the perverted man in the office, the unfair hard work, coming home to a filthy house. Rose figured out how to keep them quiet.

But Elaine had a sharp tongue, not like Audrey. Audrey was loud. Elaine was cutting. Yet Rose knew what both women wanted: to have the upper hand.

"Would you get me an ashtray, dear? And a drink?" Elaine sat down in the leather chair in the Florida room, lit her Raleigh Filter Tip, and noticed the sun-screened porch outside. "I've always wanted a sunroom. It's so nice that you have one."

Making sure he could see her, Rose fumed at Edwin as he set the luggage down in the Florida room.

Thomas walked into the kitchen. "Can an Irishman get a Highball in this house?"

"This isn't a dry county, Dad," Edwin joked from the Florida room. "Rose, make your father a Highball."

Rose tried to smile. She remembered Edwin's promises that Pierceville was a stepping stone to better things. By next year Paul would be able to help run the store, and maybe they could go see snow for Christmas. If not, Mamma and Daddy and Donald's family would visit when she hosted Thanksgiving. She'd have to hide the alcohol. The house would be dry then.

"God Dammit! Rose, I need that ashtray." Elaine's ashes dropped onto the brown leather easy chair. She wiped them off, revealing a black, coarse hole burnt into the arm. ❧

CHAPTER III

Talented and Gifted

Jacob's kindergarten teacher phoned Rose one morning and asked her to come in for a meeting. Rose was sure something wrong. Moving as if in double time, she let her house dress drop to the floor; put on her face: lipstick, rouge, eye shadow; slipped into tapestry pants adorned with yellow, white, and gold flowers; pulled on a white blouse; stepped into in heels, and cantered to the car.

She held her cheeks taught as she drove and grit her teeth. Stopping here, turning there, she paid no attention to the road; a parade of thoughts trampled through her mind to a Sousa march at high speed. Such catastrophizing happened in no other brain.

Except Jacob's.

Out of breath, Rose let herself down in the little orange chair at the kid-sized table across from Mrs. Atkins and braced herself.

Didn't they have chairs that fit a grown-up?

33

"Mrs. Murtaugh, Jacob has an excellent mind. He reads faster than other children; his comprehension exceeds expectations."

Rose fluffed her hair and cleared her throat. "Well, I'm not surprised. I figured that's what the call was about. Jacob has been reading those little board books since he was three-years-old."

"I don't think you understand," Mrs. Atkins said, "he recalls the books I read aloud word for word, even weeks later."

Rose's face bloated with pride, signifying her certainty she had imparted giftedness in her womb. "When Jacob was born, all the nurses were amazed his eyes opened so early." Rose made her eyes wide and leaned toward Mrs. Atkins when she said amazed. "They said he seemed to be looking at them, focusing on their faces. All of them told me they had never seen a baby seem so aware; those were the exact words the nurses used, Mrs. Atkins. Aware."

Rose knew Jacob would be different from other children. Thelma, Audrey's sister, prophesied of his wisdom when she first held him.

If learning was like pulling stacks of books from bookshelves and reading them, Jacob could choose several at a time, flip through them, absorb what was on the pages, retain the information, and move on to the next batch.

But his mind shut down the moment he was made to learn what he saw no value in, such as math. For the subject had to interest him. He was naturally curious about adding blocks and taking them away, yet assigning numbers felt like something had been lost, as though an opaque film had been placed between him and the world. He found counting interesting, but formulating one apple plus one apple equals two apples removed Jacob from whatever was in front of him that could be touched, heard, or smelled.

"It's only his attention span that's preventing us from placing him in the gifted program," said Mrs. Atkins.

Rose was no longer as keen on Mrs. Atkins as she had been. "Is that something he can work on?"

"Acquiring the discipline to stick with subjects even if they don't seem to directly apply would be good for him. We can have him tested again next year. There is another issue I'd like to bring up, now that we're meeting. Jacob has some challenges socially." Mrs. Atkins fingered the large, white beads on her necklace.

"He's just shy. It takes him a while to warm up," said Rose, reassuring herself if Jacob had social problems, he inherited them from Edwin.

"I have seen this before in other children. I want to recommend Jacob speak with the counselor. He's very good with—"

"Jacob is fine. I'll talk to him. You focus on teaching his lessons."

The pitapat of Rose's heels on the floor pealed through the hallway as if a single clack had been elongated, taffy-like, from Mrs. Atkins' room to the exit. As she drove home, her thoughts boiled like water; furious; afraid, angry at Jacob for making Mrs. Atkins think there was something wrong with him. Didn't he know better than to make his mother look bad? The Murtaughs were known in Pierceville. People talked. What it would mean

35

to have a child in the gifted program.

But Jacob was neither aware of his social problems, or that he was bright. But he knew he was different. What his quick mind could do with information and facts, his legs and arms could not do with a ball or a bat. He belonged to a taxon of boys lacking athletic prowess; extending a hand to a ball, unnatural; running a field of bases, absurd; kicking an object where one intends, unfathomable. Therefore, the other boys seemed strange to him; they would rather play outside at recess than learn in the classroom.

Coach Finley yelled for the boys to line up. He selected two captains; they picked their teammates. Jacob was left standing by himself, like scraggly driftwood on a lonely beach. Coach Finley told him to play the outfield.

Jacob heard the ball smack against the bat and tried to follow its arc until it blurred. The white of it against the blue sky reminded him of the soaring gulls at the gulf. He closed his eyes and smelled the salt air and felt the sea spray against his face. The shouting boys in the field became pelicans and seagulls fighting over a mullet; Coach Finley's hollering was a father running after his children splashing in the surf. Jacob looked for his mother, but could not see her. He wanted to lay his head against her breast and go to sleep.

"The ball, you idiot," some kid said.

"Boy, what's wrong with you? You've got to pay more attention," said Coach Finley. The man was also an elder at First Lutheran Church. He knew Edwin well; as duty goes, from one man to another, he would have to bring up his concerns about Jacob—such an uncoordinated boy, but the sweetest kid you'd ever meet. The sensitive type. The other boys couldn't relate to him.

"Jacob you're a fag," said one boy.

"I don't want him on my team," yelled another.

Floating back from his eye sockets, Jacob came to rest in a place deep inside his skull where life continued all around. A thick padding protected him there. It was a space where words still hurt—not because they came from someone else—but because Jacob heard the truth in this place. It was on this occasion in first grade, standing in the outfield, Jacob heard The Voice say: Nobody likes you. You're all alone.

He tried to pick up the ball. He dropped it. He picked it up again and threw it, but it landed a few feet in front of him. The scene was like living through a scary movie again and again, for he knew the ending since it happened every day.

Coach Finley was disappointed. Jacob's classmates were ashamed. All his vim to stand up for himself escaped.

You will never be like them.

He knew The Voice was right. Self-hatred settled onto him like a Kevlar vest.

The next day he told Coach Finley he forgot his dress-out clothes at home. Finley gave him a warning and made him sit next to Ms. Catherine on the bench, which Jacob wanted to do very much. She was a fifth-grade teacher. He liked to talk with her about science. He wondered how many times he could miss dressing out before coach Finley would send a note home. Mommy would be very mad.

"Are you making friends this year, Jacob?" asked Rose. The first two years of elementary school had been so lonely for him. She had to leave the furniture store at least twice a week and go to the school because Jacob cried for her. And then there were the days he was just too sick to attend: a fever, a headache, a cough. Sometimes the school nurse would call and tell Rose the child was begging to be picked up. Most of the time, she told the nurse to have him tough it out; he was faking.

"Yes, Mommy, I have lots of friends," said Jacob, following her to the laundry room, grabbing a stray brown nylon sock off the floor on the way. Mommy can't know the truth, Jacob thought. He held up the sock as a peace offering; as proof he was a good and thoughtful boy, even though he could not figure out how to make the children stop teasing him. Her back was turned and she did not notice the hand and the sock in the air. Dare he tell her he found it on the floor? That she'd dropped it? She can't know about the scary boys and how he dreaded changing clothes in front of them. She can't know he lied to Coach Finley about not having dress out shorts.

She can't know you made a mistake because it might kill her, said The Voice.

Opening and closing his fingers, Jacob made the sock speak in a high voice. "Don't forget me," the striped brown thing said.

"Throw that in, Jacob. I don't have time for games. And bring me the box of detergent out of the grocery bag in the kitchen."

Before he crossed over the gold metal strip dividing the linoleum and the carpet, he shuffled on his feet, stepping first with the right, then pushing off with the left and back to the right foot again in order to take two steps with his right foot out of the laundry room.

Right is better than left, The Voice told him. *And even is better than odd. Nothing bad will happen, for now.*

He did not like to have to lie to her, but he would, just as Mommy and Daddy had to lie to Maw Maw and Grandaddy and Nana and Papa because, "How we spend our money is none of their business."

That Jacob had to adjust to the move from Lakesville to Pierceville, and from the trailer to a house, and begin a new school and make new friends, and have a baby sister all of a sudden; Rose worried it was too much for him. And now she and Edwin would have to hire a nanny so she could help Edwin manage the furniture store. She worried he might feel abandoned even more, but everything they were doing was for the children, she told herself. Once the store was a success, they would have more time with Jacob and Melody.

But would it ever be a success? The store wasn't making enough money to bring in Paul as a partner, but Edwin promised that in a year or two Pierceville's growth would continue, Carter would probably get re-elected, and the economy would improve. But would Jacob have a normal life here? She didn't know why she asked that question. Was there a normal life?

Carrying the box of soap, Jacob shuffled his feet to step back into the laundry room on his right foot.

Right is better than left.

"Are there any little girls you like?" Rose noticed Jacob still wearing the brown sock puppet and held out her hand impatiently, for she had started the wash.

What was the right answer? Some boys had girlfriends. They passed notes to each other in class. Jacob wanted to run through the hall, out the door, around the house. Play, play, play! But all he could think about was that day in second grade, on the playground by the metal spider, when Nancy puffed out her chest and said, "I've kissed a boy. How about you, James?"

"No, I've never kissed a boy," said James. Nancy, James, and Virginia laughed. Jacob didn't. He thought about James' clean skin and tanned face. He liked his long eyelashes.

"Would you ever let a boy kiss you?" asked Nancy. James blushed and shrugged his shoulders.

"I'll kiss James," said Jacob. He liked James. He liked Nancy; she was his friend. But Jacob didn't know what she knew about kissing, or about boys and girls and what they did when the teachers weren't looking. He didn't know the rules.

But Jacob did like to look at the magazines he found last summer in Edwin's golf bag. He took one out and sat on the black leather seat of a rusting yellow riding mower in the garage. Jacob examined a man on a rock all big and hairy down there; he ran his finger along the page. Another man floated in a pond with just his toes, his face, and his thing sticking out of the water like a turtle. Taking up two pages lay a man in the center of the magazine. Out it popped; it was bigger than the other's he'd seen. Bigger than any boy at school. He passed his eyes over it again and again, until he could close his eyes and see the pink and white flesh, and the lines, and the holes, and the eyes, and the smile.

A wasp buzzed over Jacob's head. It landed on a nest in the corner above him. Daddy would be mad if he found out I looked. Mommy would be mad if she came in the garage. Jacob closed the magazine and rolled it up. The wasp flew from the nest and landed on the glass window in the door leading outside. It circled left and right, as one lost in a parking lot. Finally, the wasp crawled between a space in the glass and became trapped in the screen. "Dear Jesus, don't let the wasp get stuck," Jacob prayed. The wasp buzzed furiously. There's no hope. Jacob took a match from the utility cabinet, struck it, and lit the wasp on fire. "You should have stayed in your nest."

Jacob brought the magazine into the Florida room to show Mommy and Daddy because he was afraid they would be mad he looked.

Rose unrolled it, turned it over, set it on her lap, and told Jacob to go outside and play.

Jacob leaned over on his tippy toes and kissed James on his cheek. James smiled at Jacob. Nancy covered her mouth and squealed. "You kissed James. Ewwww."

Jacob didn't want to kiss Nancy or Virginia.

"Jacob, you didn't answer me. Who are your friends this year?"

"I have a friend named Virginia."

"What do you do with Virginia?" Rose looked up from her folding. A wave of concern crossed her face.

"We like to play house at recess."

"You play house with little girls?" Rose's forehead tensed as she creased the folded shirt on her lap. Maybe Mrs. Atkins had been right. Jacob's confession confirmed what she had dreaded all along—he wasn't going to be a normal boy. Pastor's recent sermon about the gays preparing to march on Washington, Edwin's magazines, Jacob's social problems, all these hung in her mind like grotesque paintings of disfigurement and torture. She had to watch and probe with extra severity.

"You mean you aren't playing sports with the other boys?"

Jacob had been tiptoeing around the bed. He shuffled his feet to land on the right. "Yes, when they play. They don't play every day," Jacob lied. Jacob wished it would rain and thunder every day, so recess and P.E. would be canceled.

"Are they picking you to be on their teams? You know how Mommy worries."

"They used to pick David first all the time, but now they pick me first. They always pick me first unless Coach Finley makes me captain, because I'm so good."

Rose folded and creased a shirt with extra zeal. "Jacob, Mommy is so proud of you. You better tell your Maw Maw about this when she's here for your birthday party because she wants you to make nice friends this year."

Jacob was relieved. Then a sensation settled in; numbness, like when Mommy rubbed the blue gel on his sore muscles. There was no feeling at first, only cold. Then the burning began. He had discovered pretending this way made him feel like he was not himself, and it hurt. ❧

BOY IN THE HOLE

CHAPTER IV

Zero Net Gain

Edwin promised Jacob he would be at the elementary school at ten o'clock in the morning and not a minute later. The long black hand covered up the six. The short one crawled past the nine; Jacob was already in a panic. The nine o'clock hour seemed wasted now as if it were slop issued to prisoners or to a sounder of swine.

He's not going to come. He always breaks his promise. Click teeth, nod. He'll be here. Relax.

Today Jacob would launch a model of the Space Shuttle Columbia into the sky from the middle of the playground in front of the entire school. As it floated back to earth attached to a parachute, he and his father would retrieve it as they smiled and laughed, and the children would cheer them on like in Chariots of Fire.

Nine forty-five.

"Class, please stand in a single-file line at the door. We are going to walk to the playground for a special event," said the teacher.

It was a pleasant February morning. Shards of ample green grass pushed up through the brown coppice promising the imminent arrival of spring.

The wind shouldn't be a problem on the trajectory, thought Jacob.

Ten o'clock.

He walked to the center of the playground. Hundreds of children from grades one through six encircled him at a distance. Several teachers walked around explaining the Shuttle program. They pointed at Jacob as he set the black pronged pad on the ground and affixed the metal launch rod. He could hear them say words like "NASA" and "Rockets." One said, "fuel tank" and "SRBs."

Five minutes after ten.

To buy time he fiddled with some wires and walked around the Shuttle several times appearing to check all the parts of the rocket.

"Launch it! Launch it! Launch it!" the children chanted.

There was nothing else to do. Everything was ready. Then Jacob saw Coach Finley trotting over waving his blue cap high in the air. His beefy, tan calves rubbed his red polyester shorts together. When he reached Jacob, he put both palms on his knees and said through several heavy breaths, "I'm sorry, son."

"What's wrong, Coach Finley?"

"Maybe your dad's not coming."

"What do I do? Should we scrub the launch?"

"No." Finley panted some more. "All these kids are here to see you launch this rocket. You've got to do it without him."

"But I need his help, Coach Finley."

"Let's go, son. These kids are counting on you."

Jacob walked toward the pad. Gravity seemed to increase the weight of his feet as he approached the Shuttle. He picked up the tiny black remote control which felt like it was made of lead. He spoke as loudly as he could, but his voice quivered.

"Thank you for coming today. My father was supposed to be here, but he couldn't make it. There was an emergency. We do everything together," Jacob lied. "Anyway, I hope you enjoy the launch. Let's all count down from ten…nine…eight…"

When everyone yelled, "One!" Jacob pushed the red launch button. Gray smoke puffed and dampened out after a second. The children began to jeer. Jacob fiddled with some wires. His hands were shaking.

"I'm sorry, everyone. We seem to be having technical difficulties today. Maybe the engines or the wires got wet. Sometimes this happens in a real launch."

"No, You're just a loser, Murtaugh. That's what happened," yelled a freckled-faced kid.

"Excuse me, young man! You're not to speak to my son that way."

"Dad! You made it. Did you remember to bring the extra engines?"

Edwin pulled out a packet from his tan leather blazer. "You mean these?"

"Help me replace the ones on the Shuttle."

After Edwin and Jacob switched out the engines, Jacob handed Edwin the remote control. "You do the honors, Dad." Edwin began the countdown again.

"Liftoff! We have liftoff of the Space Shuttle Columbia," yelled Jacob, jumping up and down. The children screamed and clapped. Several ran toward where they hoped the sections would land.

"Children, be careful not to step on any of the parts if you find them," cautioned a teacher.

The momentary chaos broke a fixed perspective Jacob had held for a long time: positive attention could feel powerful. And if Jacob looked at his father in a certain light, he didn't always disappear. But Jacob had to look very hard.

There must be some way to get him to care about math. Maybe there was some friendlier way, some less forceful way. But she had tried all those, thought Rose. As she looked at Jacob trembling at his desk in his room, his face apple red, his teeth clenched, she thought, perhaps, she could have done better—hired a tutor, bought some books. But she would regret nothing she had done because it was her imposing force as a mother that would make him strong.

"These answers are wrong, Jacob!" She slapped him across his face.

"I don't understand the problems, Mommy." He tried not to cry for sobbing would only make her angrier.

"Erase them and start over. This is your last chance." She left his room to heat the Swanson TV Dinners.

As Jacob erased one of the long division problems, he rubbed through the page. *Should I call her?* He froze.

"I don't hear you writing, Jacob. I'm coming in there

in five minutes."

"But Mommy, the page tore."

Rose slammed the oven shut. Her footsteps thudded down the hallway.

"You ruined your math sheet? You did this on purpose!" When she grabbed his upper arm, her nails sunk into his skin. She threw him from the desk across the room.

"You'll stay here in the dark until your father comes home."

Jacob heard the car pull into the garage. Rose opened his bedroom door, turned on the light, and held out one of Edwin's T-shirts.

"Wear this, Jacob," she said sweetly. "And if you say anything to your father about earlier, you'll get much worse. Now come to the table."

Jacob rolled his peas onto his turkey then plopped a few of them into his mashed potatoes. With each maneuver of his fork, he kept his other hand on the sleeve of his upper arm and watched for a reaction from Edwin. Rose's eyes bore into him.

"What Mom? I'm just not hungry."

"Why not, son?" Edwin asked, looking at Jacob.

He lifted his sleeve. I'm so sore from today.

Edwin noticed the nail marks and bruising, but glanced at his TV Dinner, then Rose. "Is it me, or are these dinners getting smaller?"

"I think they are. It's inflation and all," said Rose.

Jacob got up from the table and went to bed.

All Jacob wanted for his ninth birthday, and what he asked for from every person in his family, was the planet

Hoth playset from Empire Strikes Back, the Imperial Attack Base, and action figures from the movie. If there were anything to spare, he wouldn't have minded getting Darth Vader's Star Destroyer, and more carrying cases for his figures.

Both sets of grandparents, aunts and uncles, cousins, and friends came through that year, and he received most of what was on his list.

For it was through the idea of The Force, Jacob longed for the power to influence people and overcome the darkness of his life.

But at his party, Jacob learned a painful lesson in science from his father. Edwin set aside a large rectangular box. He told Jacob to save that one for last. What could be in it? he wondered, and as he opened the other gifts, and as he kissed that one on the cheek and hugged the other around the neck, and as he threw the blue and green shiny wrapping paper into the trash bag to stave off Rose's nerves at the chaotic mess, his anticipation shot up like a fever until it was time to open the gift from his father.

Jacob tore across the gift wrap like a badger, ignoring Audrey's scolding to carefully separate the paper's folds by running a fingernail along the tape so that one might reuse the paper (in this way she recycled every piece of aluminum foil, rinsing and laying it over the faucet to dry; washing every container of yogurt, butter, or whipped cream and stacking them in her shelves as if she were curating a museum of plastics).

Lifting the lid, he saw a maroon football jersey; he saw his name printed in white block letters; he saw black cleats and white socks; he saw a gray and white helmet, and he saw an athletic cup and supporter, resting like an ugly crown on top of it all. Jacob's back was to his parents. Taking several deep breaths between sobs, he stared into that box. He did not wipe the tears from his face.

How could he have done this? wondered Jacob. His father must hate him. Aware of the disappointment, aware of wanting to trash the jersey, yet having no power to do it, melancholy took him over. Instead, he sat searching for words. Should he thank his father? Jacob imagined setting the gift on fire in front of Edwin. Was the jersey a test? A message? Was it a gift a loyal son would want, and only prodigal son would reject?

After all positives and negatives have been calculated, the overall improvement is said to be the net gain. But math doesn't always meet one's expectations. In Quantum Physics, the addition of a thing to another thing can result in zero net gain. The devastating depth of Edwin's misunderstanding of his son sent Jacob to that padded place behind his eyes where he could hear The Voice: *Even your father doesn't understand you. You are alone.* Jacob failed the test and had failed Edwin. Therefore, there was no point in ever trying to please him.

When he stopped crying, Jacob stood and pivoted towards Edwin as his composure clicked into place like a magical pair of ruby slippers, transporting him from the land of disenchantment to the world of insouciance.

Jacob put all the jersey parts back in the box and stomped past his father.

"This jersey is never gonna leave this box, ever." Then he ran to his room and slammed the door. ❧

AKIVA HERSH

CHAPTER V

Unto Us A Child Is Born

Jacob heard the car door. Audrey jumped from the couch and told him to wait in the purple bedroom. The white linens on the four-post mahogany bed were cast in lavender light from the sun filtering through the curtains reflecting off the purple walls. Except for the brass ticking clock hanging on the wood-paneled walls over the large television in the living room, the house was quiet. Jacob knelt on the lavender-blue carpet and folded his hands. "God, please let my sister be just like me and let us be friends. Help me to take care of her. Amen."

The back door opened. The sounds of Audrey's murmuring and fussing bounced through the house like the chime of a cuckoo clock. Suddenly, Jacob's mother and father brought a bundle into the room. Something clean and sweet tinged the air like the smell of a forest after a rain. Edwin knelt beside Jacob. Rose leaned over him and placed a pink clump beneath Jacob's face. Everything was pink: the linens, her hat, her flesh, everything except her eyes—all blue—which opened for a moment to take in Jacob.

"This is your baby sister, Melody," said Rose.

"Melody." Jacob repeated her name like a prayer. "I love her already." He scooped his hands under her and picked her up. She smelled new. This is what new life smells like, thought Jacob. This is the smell of sister.

Cold tendrils released from around his stomach as he watched her; someone had arrived to share his life, his laughter, his loneliness, his fears. *This is my sister.*

"Be careful with her, Jacob," said Rose, propping up Melody's head.

"I am. I will protect her. She's going to be my best friend, and I'll take her with me wherever I go." He put his pinkie finger in her Lilliputian palm; her fingers curled around as if the siblings had made a promise.

Audrey cooed, "Isn't that so sweet. They are so precious together. Look, Klaus."

"It's real sweet," he managed to say.

In Pierceville, the rush of life engulfed Rose the way the sea and sand ooze into a footprint soon after the foot is withdrawn. Her parents and in-laws didn't come around to help; Edwin returned to work; the baby needed feeding and diapering; Jacob was hungry; homework and laundry piled up; the house had to be cleaned. Life didn't stop for Rose. She felt as though she was a passenger on a train careening off track, heading for a ravine and no way to warn anyone.

She knew she couldn't have seen it. But everything in her compelled her to tell what her eyes saw. It was a horror, whether if what she saw was true, or if it was a figment. If it was true, she had to warn Jacob; she had to protect him if she had the strength. If it wasn't, she needed him to get help.

"Jacob, get under this table with me right now," Rose yelled. Jacob was playing in his room. *Where was the other one?* She'd just seen it...

"Jacob come here. We're not safe."

"What's wrong, Mommy? Why are you under the dining room table?"

"I saw the baby coming down the hall to get me."

"Mommy, where's Melody?"

"I don't know. I'm so sorry." Rose rocked back and forth, holding Jacob to her breast.

"Mommy, I'm going to go look for Melody."

He squirmed away from her and ran down the hallway. The baby was in her room, lying in her bassinet working up to a cry. She needed to be changed.

"Come here, sweet girl, I've got you." He smiled at her and held her close to his cheek. "Let's go see Mommy."

Jacob crawled under the table again. "See? She's not going to hurt you. She's just stinky."

"I know, son. Mommy is so sorry. You're my good boy." Rose took Melody and rocked her. "Bring me the phone. I need to call your daddy."

Rose phoned Edwin and told him the baby had come down the hallway to kill her. He thought she was joking until Rose shrieked. Jacob grabbed the phone.

"Daddy, please come home. I'm scared."

Over Rose's wailing, Edwin heard Melody crying.

"We're under the table, Daddy."

"I'll be home just as soon as I can, son."

"Where are you taking me, Edwin?"

"We're going to see Dr. Berel. He's going to meet us at Lakesville Memorial."

"Are they going to lock me up? They're going to put me away, and you're going to take my children, aren't you?"

"Honey, we're just going to get you some help. Something is wrong. Try and relax."

She'd been telling him for weeks something was wrong. It took the baby trying to attack her to peel Edwin Murtaugh's attention off that damn store, like an old window decal refusing to come off the glass. He doesn't lift a finger at home; puts the car in the garage, expects dinner, turns on the TV looking for a sports game; doesn't even acknowledge his wife and children. What did he expect to happen? All he cares about is football and that store.

Rose could not stop fuming. She was sure Tommy's wife Linda had help when Emily was born; probably had a maid, had someone to cook and clean. They got a visit from Elaine and Tom Sr. too; they stayed with them for a couple of weeks. But did they lift a finger to help with Jacob or Melody?

"No, but Mother and Daddy help us in their own way," said Edwin. "Look, let's not get into this now. You're upsetting yourself even more." There was no winning an argument when she was like this. Edwin could never understand why she looked for every injustice, every wrong; she could never forgive the smallest mistake, she always held a grudge. Yet if she messed up, she expected everyone to overlook it. The Baptists were so full of judgment; she would never get the poison out of her system, no matter how far he took her from them.

Rose's doctors ran a panel of tests: blood work, x-rays, an MRI and agreed she needed to be admitted to the psychiatric wing.

Dr. Berel called Edwin into his office. He didn't look at Edwin. He removed a paperclip from the labs, fidgeted with papers, then pushed his thick, black glasses up the hook on his nose.

"What's wrong with my wife, Dr. Berel?"

"Edwin we could be looking at ovarian cancer. The next step is exploratory surgery."

Cancer. The next thought was death, and then the children, and then the store, and then—Edwin sighed a deep breath—was that the feeling of freedom? And then the guilt.

"Okay, I want to talk to her about it."

"She's not able to consent. Her state of mind isn't there. I need you to sign these forms to authorize the surgery. We need to do it now."

Like strata in the layers of rock, or rings in a tree trunk, one's decisions and choices lay down detectable lines throughout our lives, one after the other. When examined, these lines reveal a landscape of who we are in totality, yet the picture is oblique, it is bare but concealed; waiting to be interpreted by a trained observer. These threads go far back to the very initial split of the first cell of our being. Several cells split, and there are blood cells. More divide and there are nerve cells and the heart. More division: the brain, the spine, the kidneys. Thousands upon thousands of divisions later come the arms, the legs, the nails, and the genitals.

Among the divisions, Rose consumed her twin sister. Perhaps it was an act of mercy, for she knew the monsters waiting for them. Or maybe it was murder, for she could sense the heartless mother carrying them both; there would not be enough love for two, and Rose was a survivor. Or maybe it was simply an opportunity, for another life existed nearby, and she needed warmth and nutrients, so she took what belonged to her. And this was how she learned to survive for the rest of her life.

After the surgery, Dr. Berel brought Edwin and Audrey into his office. Edwin tried to comprehend the implication Rose had a twin that formed into a cyst on top of her ovary.

"Dermoid cyst is the accurate term," Dr. Berel said.

"So Audrey was carrying twins?" Edwin asked. "And Rose basically ate it?"

"That's rather crude, Edwin. What we removed today was like a twin," said Dr. Berel, glancing at Audrey to see if she understood.

As if trying to wipe the image away, Audrey shook her head from side to side. She put up her hand. "I can't believe this. This is ungodly. I knew something was wrong with her the day she was born, but you've got it all wrong."

"Mrs. Ramburg, I asked you into my office to find out if you had known of any history of—"

"No, there's no history of anything, and you're wrong. I never had no other baby inside me. I want a second opinion."

"I'm afraid it's a little late for that. We've already removed the tissue and—"

"I want to see it. I want to see the baby."

"It's not quite a baby, Mrs. Ramburg."

"I don't care. Let me see it."

Audrey insisted Rose look at it, too. It had hair, some nails, teeth, and a single eye; it was a hideous mass of flesh the size of an adult finger.

Rose carried on about knowing all her life some part of her was missing. Audrey went into hysterics, slapping Rose across the face.

"They're going to get rid of this thing today, and we're not going to speak another word of it, you hear me?"

"Yes, ma'am."

After Audrey left, Rose mourned. Dr. Berel made a referral for follow-up therapy for Rose and Edwin. He recommended they go at least once a week to help with the postpartum depression and to deal with the loss.

Exactly a week after Rose was released from Lakesville Memorial, Edwin, Rose, Jacob, and Melody drove into Tampa to meet June, Rose's new therapist. The family walked into a large room where husbands and wives sat in hard, plastic chairs arranged in a circle. Jacob hid behind Edwin, grasping his coat jacket as they walked.

Jacob was the only child in the group. June invited him to play on a mat in the corner and gave him crayons and coloring books. He pretended to be interested in coloring but listened to the couples talk about being sad and mad. Why were they sad and mad about having a baby? Jane told a woman to hit a pillow and yell at it like it was her husband. Covering his ears, Jacob inched further into the corner; he wanted to leave. He looked at Rose's face as she fell through a trap door in her mind and drifted down a tunnel where it was impossible to follow. Her vacant expression appeared as though one had flipped the switch on a television, the light fading to a singular white point, then all that remained was blackness.

Rose was holding Melody loosely. Jacob remembered her newness in that purple room, the excitement, his new best friend. Rose took that from him. He was all alone again. ⚜

CHAPTER VI

This Is My Body

Jacob dreaded twilight. Dinner, shower, TV, a bedtime story—all bells tolling the arrival of the dark. Comfort came not in a blanket, a nightlight, a stuffed animal, but in his longing to feel God. When the dark came Jacob, abandoned in his room, surveyed the aphotic terrain of lumpy sheets, adumbral shapes, and black space like a lone astronaut lost and far from his craft. In this emptiness, thoughts of Heaven and the angels kept him from sinking into the thick space behind his eyes where he heard The Voice.

His final precaution, every night before switching off the light, was to turn through the thin pages of his Bible (the Red Letter Edition). To Jacob, Holy Scripture was better than comics or Choose Your Own Adventure books because the stories were real, and Jesus seemed to speak directly to him. For he knew by some mysterious bodily impression, a settling in his gut, the Divine was present.

Passing by his room one night and seeing the light on, Rose stood at the door. "You have a special connection with God, Jacob."

"Why, Mommy?"

"You have an unusual faith. It's hard for people to believe in something they can't see."

"Do you have an unusual faith?" Jacob asked.

"I just want to be with Jesus. I'm ready."

The world is an evil place. Why won't God just take me? Rose wondered. Why let me suffer so?

She looked at Jacob on the bed sitting cross-legged in his Superman Underoos. She didn't see a small boy but an intermediary between herself and God.

I'm special because I brought Jacob into the world.

"God will reward you for your faith. But only if you're a good boy and honor your mother and father. Especially your mother. I need you, Jacob. God gave you to me to take care of me until I die. Look at the way Jesus took care of Mary. Do you understand?"

"How will God reward me?" asked Jacob, tracing the outline of the Dead Sea on a map.

"God listens to you more than most children. You prayed for a sister, and you got one. Whenever you pray for people to get better, they do, especially when you pray for me. Will you pray for me, Jacob? Will you say a prayer for Mommy right now?"

Jacob thought she could be right because he asked God every night not to let his parents die while he slept, and for God not to let his house burn down. For he was terrified of that on account of hearing about the neighbors across the highway who lost their house to a fire and had to go live in a shelter.

"I'll pray for you before I go to sleep."

"Pray for me now, out loud. I need to hear you."

An ugly feeling erupted in Jacob's stomach; hot, stinging, heaving, like when he had to pull his underwear down and cough for the doctor.

"Don't you love your mother? Get on your knees and fold your hands."

She knelt beside Jacob. He whispered to God over her sobs.

Later, recalling what his mother had said about faith, Jacob wondered why God let houses catch fire. And how come bad men hijacked airplanes in the Middle East. And why did people have to get sick and die? And why hadn't Jesus come back to fix all the problems? And if Jesus was supposed to return any moment, like the Bible said, why weren't people getting ready for him? And why did Daddy bother going to work to sell furniture? And why were people even buying furniture?

He asked his nanny, Jean Ann, about these things, but she said she was a Baptist, and he should speak to his father.

"Why are there Baptists and Catholics and Lutherans?" asked Jacob. "How did all these religions get started?"

"People believe different things," answered Edwin.

"But why? What can't we all believe the same thing?"

"I don't know, son. One day it will all make sense, and everyone will believe same thing."

"What about the people who don't believe in Jesus? Do they go to hell?"

"God will deal with them," said Edwin.

"Jesus says they're going to hell. Mommy says Nana and Papa are going to hell because they're Catholics. Is that true?"

"No, they're not going to hell."

No one ever had good answers. In the fifth grade, Jacob attended classes at Our Savior Lutheran to learn about the sacrament of Holy Communion. Boys bounced and wiggled in the metal chairs. Girls played with their hair and tittered over Olivia Newton-John's hit, *Physical*. Jacob waited for Pastor Motz to arrive. He placed his pencil parallel to the notebook, an inch away. When the boy next to Jacob slammed his elbow against the table, the pencil went rolling. Jacob returned it to its former spot, having noted the distance from the notebook to the edge of a black faux knot in the plastic tabletop.

"Peace of the Lord be with you," said Pastor Motz, carrying a notepad of foolscap and a large print leather-bound Bible, his gait giving out an air of affection and humility.

"And also with you," muttered the children.

Pastor Motz surveyed the children with his blue infant eyes which seemed to float, unfastened, behind his silver-rimmed glasses, so that like an infant, they only reflected an openness to the world, but gave no intimation of wanting anything.

"Last week we spoke about the Exodus from Egypt. Today we will speak about Jesus' body and—"

Jacob raised his hand. "Pastor Motz, how do the bread and wine become Jesus?"

"It happens because God makes it so," Pastor Motz

said as if bread and wine turning into flesh and blood was the most natural thing in the world.

"But they look the same."

"Of course they do. The sacraments are a sign Jesus is with us at that moment. So it was important for God to allow us to recognize them."

"But Jesus said he would always be with us. And he said to have the bread and wine once a year, not every week." Nagging doubt, like molten lead pouring down his throat, burned through Jacob's stomach.

"He is always with us," said Pastor Motz. "But this is a special meal, a special time to be with the Lord."

"Then why—"

Pastor Motz smiled down at Jacob. "You have very good questions. Hard questions. But I think if we read on, things will become clearer to you."

God is a fairy tale, said The Voice.

Jacob remembered the day in fourth grade he found out Santa wasn't real. The Voice had warned him then, too. Rose was combing his hair to look nice for the picture with Melody and Santa at the mall.

"How can Santa fly to all the malls and take pictures with all the children and still deliver presents on time?"

"Jacob, you're almost ten-years-old. You should've figured it out by now. Mommy and Daddy are Santa." Rose shellacked another layer of extra-hold Dippity-Do gel over Jacob's cowlick.

Jacob began to cry. Rose popped him with the brush on top of his head. "Don't you ruin this for your sister. She's too young."

If Santa was a lie, maybe Jesus was also, thought

Jacob. On the way to the mall, Jacob counted his doubts like rosary beads, pausing over each one to pray for forgiveness.

The Ramburgs and the Murtaughs would come on Sunday to watch him eat the little round wafer and drink wine from the tiny clear cup. He hoped he didn't get drunk, or want to spit it out. He did not like the wine Nana and Daddy drank. Nor did he like Papa's Highballs.

The plan was for everyone to celebrate at the restaurant at Holiday Inn, a favorite of Edwin and Rose's because it seemed elegant enough for Elaine and Thomas Murtaugh, but not overly priced for Audrey and Klaus Ramburg.

Jacob did not understand why they were celebrating with a special lunch and giving him gifts. First communion isn't a birthday party. Pastor Motz said this was a chance to be close to Jesus in a special way and to be forgiven of sins. "It would be the start of a new relationship with God," he said.

Mommy said Maw Maw and Grandaddy might act a little strange because they believe communion is only a reminder of Jesus's suffering and death, and Baptists didn't do it as often as the Lutherans. Did the Lutherans overdo it? How could Jesus' followers disagree about something so important as holy communion? He felt like he was standing on a slippery inflatable raft in the middle of a pool.

"You're a Lutheran," Rose declared, "and you're going to take communion like every other Lutheran." She wouldn't put up with Jacob's questions today. For she had enough of her own to worry about; her parents and Edwin's parents were breaking bread together. What if Elaine cussed, ordered a drink, lit a cigarette? What if Tom Sr. made an off-colored joke? She took Jacob by the arm. "Be prepared, Nana and Papa may be uncomfortable too."

"Why? Do they believe something different from us and Maw Maw and Grandaddy about Jesus and communion?"

"Edwin," Rose nudged him with her elbow as if to say, *You're the former Catholic. This is on you.*

"Catholics believe the wafer becomes Jesus' actual body, and the wine turns into his actual blood. It's called transubstantiation."

"Do you believe that, Daddy?"

"No."

"You used to believe it?"

"Yes, I was taught about it in catechism."

"None of your grandparents will take communion with you, Jacob." Rose didn't try to conceal her triumph. Raising a Lutheran son was an act of rebellion she was proud of—Klaus and Audrey couldn't make her choose a religion, or a husband—and she got to be hurt and indignant over the Murtaughs disapproval for not raising her children as Catholics.

As a bonus, she could take a stab at Edwin for hiding behind his religion when they were dating in high school. Rose had wanted to go further than hand-jobs when they parked in the orchards, but he played the part of the good catholic boy. She knew something was off. It was not until trying to conceive Jacob did she suspect what it was.

"And you will never be able to take communion at either of your grandparents' churches because you don't believe what they believe," said Rose, fixing Jacob's brow hair along the part. "Basically both the Baptists and the Catholics think we're all going to Hell."

"Rose, you don't have to spell it out for him."

"Why not? It's the truth."

All of it made Jacob wither. He hoped God would accept him when he knelt at the altar to receive Jesus; he prayed for a sign.

Posed, the family sat stiffly around the table at the Holiday Inn, a caricature of Da Vinci's Last Supper. Jacob walked from the bathroom to the open seat between Edwin and Rose, the place of honor. Rose checked her makeup in her round, brass compact. Edwin struck his wine glass three times with his fork.

"And here's to the man of the hour," Edwin raised the glass and smiled at his son without looking at him. He had a way of being aware of Jacob but never seeing him.

Thomas Senior roared, "Cheers." Elaine clinked glasses with Jacob. Audrey smiled and raised her glass of tea. Klaus sat expressionless, like a figure of a soldier from a distant time in a wax museum; the kind that scared children because he looked lifelike enough he might spring into action and gut them for getting too close.

"Cheers, Bubba." Melody raised her Shirley Temple to toast her big brother. "Let's pretend to play communion with my tea set when we get home," Melody whispered. "You be the pastor and give me some pretend wine. We can use juice."

"When everyone leaves the house, but not before," Jacob cautioned.

From her creme leather purse, Elaine took out a long, skinny box covered in mother-of-pearl wrapping paper, topped with a red bow. "Open it, Jay. Papa and I are so proud of you."

Jacob opened the box. Inside was a gold chain with a gold cross. Jesus was not hanging on it; Jacob was relieved. He liked it very much.

"I hope the length is okay. The gold is fourteen carats," said Elaine.

"Thank you, it's so nice," said Jacob, hugging Elaine, then Thomas Sr.

"That is just gorgeous, Elaine," said Audrey. "You have such good taste. And look, it's the perfect length for his neck. Here, baby, this is from Maw Maw and Grandaddy."

Audrey proudly handed him a blue envelope, as if in competition. He stood next to her, leaning against her chair as he opened it. The front of the card showed a little boy, aged three or four, in his pajamas kneeling by the bed praying. When Jacob opened the card, a one-hundred-dollar bill fell out.

"We weren't sure what to get you so we thought you could get something you'd like."

"Thank you, Maw Maw." He hugged her tightly and tried to kiss her on the cheek, but she turned her mouth to meet his lips like she always did. Her mouth was mushy and wet, and she made sucking noises when she kissed him. Jacob embraced Klaus. He smiled and said woodenly, "We love you, son." Then, like an animatronic figure whose plug had been pulled, he returned to his motionless, disapproving posture.

Rose slid a small white box with a brown bow toward Jacob. "This is from Mommy and Daddy," she said.

Jacob opened the box. Gleaming gold, he removed the handsome ring. The band was thick; a cross and ichthus design encircled it, the first ring he had ever owned. A magic amulet, he thought.

"I love it! Which finger should I wear it on?"

"I thought you might wear it on the ring finger of your right hand. I hope it fits."

Rose sold costume jewelry and had sample cases in her bedroom closet. Just weeks ago, before a sales convention in Dallas, she took them out to polish them. She had noticed Jacob trying on various women's rings until he eyed one with the cross and fish.

"It fits. Thank you, Mommy and Daddy."

He looked around the table at his family being careful to think a good thought, nod his head, and click his teeth before he moved on to the next person. For The Voice had taught him this was how he could protect people. His grandparents were smiling. His parents were holding hands. Even Melody spoke nicely to him (except for when she made fun of his clicking and nodding). No one argued; everyone had attended church as one family; the Ramburgs and Murtaughs celebrated at the same table, and on that day, in front of them all, he had been forgiven of his sins; he had taken inside of him the symbol of the presence of Lord. The peace and togetherness in his family was the sign from God he'd prayed for.

Audrey suggested Jacob bless God for the meal. As he led them all in prayer, a feeling deep within his belly began to rise, ballooning up to his chest, then ascending to his eyes. He was afraid the feeling would turn to tears, but when he finished his prayer and focused on his surroundings, he found his bearings, as though he had been floating above his head while at the same time tuned in to the inner workings of his mind.

He heard a voice: *"You belong to me, and you are mine."* He knew this was God. He knew because of the special day, and the special occasion, and maybe the special ring he wore. His family came together because of him, and this made Jesus happy, and so Jacob was happy. He belonged to Jesus, and like Peter, maybe Jesus was calling him to work for him. Jacob began to realize he was special, after all.

Before he fell asleep that night, Rose came into his room. She was holding a blue book with a seagull on it and a card in a turquoise envelope.

"Jaqueline Gregory, Mommy's friend in the choir, handed me this gift for you this morning. She wants you to read her card first, then she said it's very important you read the whole book. She said you're such a wise soul, so you'll get it."

Jacob opened the card.

Dear Jacob,

God loves you very much. He can be found in many places, sometimes even in a church! But He is everywhere, and I think you already know He's not only in a building.

Keep searching. Always ask your thousand questions even if it drives your parents, your teachers, and your pastors nuts. Don't be afraid to be who you are. Be like Jonathan Livingston Seagull. If you want to talk about what you find when you start to fly, you can always talk to me.

Love,
Jaqueline

Jacob stayed up very late reading about the sea bird who was not like the rest of his flock. Jonathan was unsatisfied living only for his daily portion of fish; there had to be more to life. When the bird discovered the thrill of flying, the other gulls turned away from him, just like the boys and girls had done to Jacob at school.

Jacob read how Jonathan discovered a teacher who taught him the flying secrets. After the seagull became the best flyer there was, he wanted to help others learn.

I want to know the secrets and be like Jonathan. Jacob felt deep inside he had the power to do it, but he needed to find a teacher to show him how. ❦

CHAPTER VII

Playing With Fire

"Don't hit the thing that'll make her pregnant," said Lena.

Carol Alice lay on her back, spreading her legs so that her knees touched the floor; her striped pink and white panties gathered at her ankles. Except for colored lights radiating from a large green ceramic Christmas tree (a handmade gift from Audrey), the living room was dark. Tiny plastic bulbs dotting each branch cast orange, red, green, blue, and yellow spots on the walls and floor. Christmas was over, New Years had passed, but Jacob's cousins left out the decorations far too long, like a corpse at a viewing, overdue for burial.

Lena shined the flashlight on Carol Alice as she spread open her labia.

"Go deep inside with your finger," Carol Alice instructed.

Jacob did not want to put his finger in there. A red and pink blossom, glistening; the smell made him turn

AKIVA HERSH

away. His vision blurred. Suddenly, as if adding weight to a balance scale, the load shifted; the scale tipped; equilibrium lost; the scale crashed and clanked under the weight of a singular impression. He did not want this.

Carol Alice was eleven, and Lena was nine. They had more experience than Jacob (who was nearly eleven) for the girls had been playing a few years with their cousin Mark. Only months ago, while they were all at Maw Maw and Grandaddy's house for a birthday party, Carol Alice announced Mark had stuck his "thing" inside her.

Jacob would not do that.

But Carol Alice and Lena persuaded Jacob to run through the house, down the hall, declaring the purple bedroom closet home-free from the terrible monster. Lena and Jacob made it in, unscathed.

"You know she's gonna find you," taunted Lena. "And then you know what she's gonna do."

"Even if she does, we're safe in the closet." Jacob pressed himself against the back wall.

Lena cupped her hand to her mouth. "He's in here," the little imp cried out.

Carol Alice slammed the bedroom door closed and turned the closet knob. Jacob squealed. Her face appeared gray and distorted.

"Since I found you, you have to do what I say," said Carol Alice. She pulled her panties down and raised her dress. "Touch your thing to mine."

"I don't want to," said Jacob.

"Do it, or I'll tell my daddy you put your thing in me, and you made me do it with you."

In the closet, Audrey's church clothes hung stiff and

78

orderly like soldiers at attention. Jacob touched the tip of his head to her hairless vagina. In the closet, crowded with pantsuits and jackets, and hats and suitcases, and shelves of cremes and scarves and bobbles and rings, Jacob heard the people laughing, each as if by themselves, at themselves, at each other. One laughed in the kitchen, leaning against a counter; another from the family room, sitting on the sofa; another roared over the drone of the TV in the living room. Each laughed violently, with fervor, as if to hide the breaking sound of their lives, no matter if it drowned the suffering laugh of another. Their gaping mouths darkened like caves, their eyes puffed in the frenzy, their fingers ripped at their throats as they laughed madly.

Jacob pulled up his pants.

"I did it. Now let's get out of here before someone comes," he said.

"Why don't you like it?" asked Lena. "Mark does. His gets real big, and he puts it all the way in there."

Jacob didn't have an answer in the closet in the purple bedroom. He didn't have an answer on the living room floor of Uncle Donald's house in the middle of the night, amongst the decaying decorations, as Carol Alice was spreading her labia and Lena was watching.

"Look at it closer. Kiss it," Carol Alice said. Jacob bent his head towards her. The smell was like sour milk.

"No, I can't."

"Then pull your pants down and get on top of me."

Making sure no one was coming, Jacob looked down the hall toward the bedrooms, then pulled down his pants and crawled on top of Carol Alice. Her warm stomach was like a heating pad, but had he not thought, emphatically, he did not want this? Had he not, in the moment of exploration, admitted: This is not me?

"Act like you're makin' a baby," Lena said, smiling and thrusting her hips.

"I don't know how," said Jacob.

"Put your thing on me and rub your body up and down," said Carol Alice.

Jacob obeyed.

No longer feeling himself moving, no longer in his body, or in the room, the red letters of Jesus flashed in his mind: "If you hold to my teaching, you are really my disciples. Then you will know the truth, and the truth will set you free." Carol Alice moaned. Jacob thought about Jesus walking on the Sea of Galilee. He imagined he was in a boat, caught in a storm. Her hips pressed up against his. Jesus walked out on the lake to save him. Then the smell of her pulled him back to the living room.

"We have to stop. This makes Jesus upset," said Jacob.

Carol Alice pushed him off and pulled up her panties. "What do you know about Jesus? You're a Lutheran, and all Lutherans are going to Hell. Only Baptists get to go to Heaven." Carol Alice turned to her sister. "Ain't that right, Lena?"

"Yeah, Jesus only saves Baptists," Lena said. "Besides, we ain't doin' nothin' wrong."

Jacob and Shawn were in the fifth grade. They didn't run in the same circles. Shawn was athletic and popular; Jacob was an introvert. The first time Jacob noticed him,

Shawn was strolling from the playground to the ball field. Jacob squinted to get a good look. Shawn's pasty white shins and curvy calves had begun to sprout fine black hairs that didn't lay flat.

I'm going to get caught staring, thought Jacob. But he couldn't look away; those legs answered questions he didn't know he had.

One Saturday afternoon, in the backyard of the house that was cater-cornered to the Murtaughs' home (a house that reminded Jacob of the horror at Amityville) Jacob saw Shawn squatting on his knees cutting grass with a pair of clippers.

"Why are you doing it like that?" Jacob asked.

Stabbing the clippers into the ground and gazing at the tall grass, Shawn said, "My dad doesn't have a lawnmower."

His palms were a pale yellow color; his fingers slender and bony.

"I have one. You could borrow it. Or I can mow it for you." *Was that weird? Will he think I'm a freak?*

"If you mow my yard, I'll teach you to slam a ball past second base."

After Jacob cut the grass, Shawn grabbed a ball and bat, and they walked shoulder to shoulder to the field across the street from Jacob's house. Out of the blue, Shawn's arm fell around Jacob's neck.

The field had once been a fairway on the nine-hole public golf course. Yellow and white butterflies exploded from weeds where they stepped. Tall, Y-shaped Bahia seeds gently slapped at their legs.

I'm going to look like an idiot. I should have left you

alone. You're a jock, and I'm a clumsy nerd. This is never going to work.

"You grip a bat like this," Shawn stepped behind Jacob and wrapped his arms around him, pressing his tummy and waist against Jacob's body. "Put your hands on top of mine," said Shawn. He drew the bat around the side of Jacob's head and rested his chin on Jacob's left shoulder.

Don't move away from me. I won't move a muscle unless you tell me to.

"We're going in slow motion."

Take all the time you want.

"Pretend like you're watching the ball." Their arms swung with one fluid movement, the bat scuffing the sky then coming to rest poised on the horizon. Jacob felt every second as if it happened frame by frame.

"How did that feel?" asked Shawn, directly into Jacob's ear.

Like coming home. "I think we need to do it again, just in case," said Jacob, playing off a shiver as though the warm April breeze gave him a chill.

Jacob kept mowing Shawn's lawn, baseball lessons became football practice, which turned into kickball instruction. They became secret friends. They listened to Michael Jackson, copying down lyrics and singing them to each other. They biked to the 7-Eleven to buy Slurpees and play Donkey Kong until the sunset. But the deal remained: at school, Jacob had to pretend not to know him.

One Friday, Shawn asked if he could spend the night. Shawn in the bed—a giddy lightness came over Jacob.

How insignificant Jacob felt next to him. He, vigorous, absorbed; Jacob, repressed, robotic; he, gregarious and unbound, Jacob, afraid and astringent; he, engaged, included; Jacob, left out, alone, and desperate. Even if it was a mistake, Jacob replied like a beggar:

"Yes, please."

Shawn sat on Jacob's bed and looked through his Star Wars card collection.

"Think your parents are asleep yet?"

"Probably," said Jacob.

"Does your dad have any dirty magazines?"

"They have a book called The Joy of Sex."

"Get it and bring it here."

Jacob found the book high on a shelf in a hall closet. On the way back, he peeked into his parent's room. The television flashed blue and white lights across his mother's face as she slept. The bathroom fan hummed loudly (for Rose needed white noise to fall asleep). Edwin was lying with his back to the door, loudly snoring.

"Got it," said Jacob, showing off the book's cover.

"Do you have any candles?"

"Yeah, why?" asked Jacob.

"To give us more light."

Jacob found a blue candle in the bathroom. It smelled like the ocean. He lit it and set it next to his bed. Shawn lifted the sheets for Jacob to crawl in. He wore a white T-shirt and briefs.

"You don't wear pajamas?" asked Jacob.

Shawn laughed. "Pajamas are for little kids. Take off your shorts and shirt." The boys huddled next to each other in their underwear, carefully flipping through The

Joy of Sex until they came to a picture of the male anatomy.

"It's still too dark," said Shawn.

Jacob went to his closet and took out a toy lightsaber. He unscrewed the long white plastic tube and turned the black hilt into a flashlight. He shined the beam in Shawn's face.

"Perfect. Now get back here."

Thunder rumbled over the roof like a large truck barreling down the road. Shawn inched closer to Jacob and pretended to be scared.

"It says the size of the average penis is about the length of a man's foot," read Jacob.

Shawn grabbed his underwear. "Mine's gonna get bigger than that."

Out of the corner of his eye, Jacob tried to look at Shawn's crotch. Then he looked at the man's penis in the book.

"But mine doesn't look like that guy's thing," said Shawn. "I'm not circumcised."

Jacob wanted to slip his hand into Shawn's underwear. He almost couldn't hold back the urge to reach out, like when he saw candy on the shelf in the kitchen that made his mouth water.

"Look, it's getting bigger." And it was.

Jacob pointed the flashlight at Shawn's underwear. "What would you do if a girl was here right now?" asked Jacob.

"We'd be doin' this," Shawn pumped his waist in the air, bouncing his rear end off the bed.

"Just a second," said Jacob. "Let me fix the light, so it's right." Jacob crawled between Shawn's legs and rested his left hand on Shawn's toned belly. He brought the large hole of the hilt over the top of his bulge. "Now, do it again," said Jacob. Shawn humped the light beam harder until he hit the top of the flashlight. "You could stick it in there if it would fit," Jacob said.

Shawn tried to push himself into the hole. "My dick is too big."

The playful look on his face suggested, *Put your hand here. I don't mind.* And as one extends a hand in greeting or the way a reflex moves the arm to catch a falling object, Jacob closed his fingers around his friend and tried to make the bulge fit in the flashlight.

Both knew it was a ruse; Jacob fumbled, dropped the flashlight and kept rubbing up and down over Shawn's briefs.

"If I take it out, maybe it will fit."

"Go ahead," Shawn said.

Jacob pretended he was trying to put it in the tube.

"Forget the flashlight."

The air shifted. Suddenly Jacob felt anything was possible. He licked the tip and searched Shawn's eyes for approval. Shawn sighed and leaned back on the pillow, both hands behind his head. Jacob traced his fingertips across Shawn's chest as he took him inside his mouth, like a sacrament.

Shawn fell asleep with his arm lying across Jacob. Jacob loved the smell of his neck and armpits. *This is what a boy smells like.*

He did not leave his body, or think of Jesus, or consider he might go to Hell. He lay in the dark savoring the taste of his friend as he put his hand inside Shawn's underwear, unable to sleep, for he had to assure himself of what had happened between them. What was this sin? Carol Alice made him feel ugly and alien. But with Shawn, he felt like himself.

Like who I really am.

"Goodnight, Shawn." Jacob rolled over. His eyes met the aloof face of Jesus on a placard that hung above him. He stared shamefully at the glow-in-the-dark cross beneath the Lord, a beacon of all the suffering and torture. While the rain fell through the night, seeping through the spring grass deep into the soil, Jacob whispered the Lord's prayer.

Melody had been spending her summer vacation with Audrey and Klaus in the Blue Ridge Mountains while Jacob stayed a few weeks with Elaine and Tom. The grandparents gave the children something to do, experiences strung together in a long, drawn-out summer, like one popped kernel thread next to the other, left to stale on a green fir tree among the tinsel and lights. It was all so predestined. Jacob wished for spontaneity to free him from the stifling amber-gold afternoon air.

On this day, he loitered by the nicotine-stained, yellow rotary phone in the kitchen while Elaine spoke to Edwin.

"I see. Is that right? When will she be back?" She covered the receiver with her free hand and smiled at Jacob. A Raleigh smoldered between her fingers; the ash was longer than what remained of the cigarette. "Run along, Jay. I'll catch up, and we'll play a card game when I'm off with your father." Chips in her shiny mauve nails revealed nicotine stains. But Jacob loved to see her skinny fingers and long nails.

"What's wrong, Nana?" he asked, leaning closer to the phone.

"...wants to come home. She was crying hysterically for her mommy to come get her," he heard Edwin say.

Melody was almost six. Jacob remembered his first trip away from home. He flew to Miami by himself for the weekend to visit his Uncle Dennis, Edwin's younger brother. Dennis treated him to dinner at Benihana (where Dennis was a manager). The knives clinking; the onions sizzling; the fire flashing brought a feeling of revelry and celebration over Jacob. After, they went to a Superman movie, then to a toy store where Dennis let Jacob pick out an expensive Star Wars gift. They played board games, cards, went swimming. Jacob didn't want to leave for he felt wonderfully wooed and considered the entire weekend one long tryst.

The only time Jacob felt out of place was when he was in the bath, and several men knocked at Dennis's door.

"Surprise," they yelled. "We're here for some fun! We have party favors."

He crept out of the bathroom wearing his towel and peered at the men. None of them wore shirts, and their jean shorts were all cut ragged and very short.

"Shh, you guys. My nephew is here, and he doesn't know about me or—anything. You can't come in. You can't even be here. I'll let you know when he's gone."

"Nephew," one of them squealed. "How old is he?"

"He's a little kid. Now skedaddle." Dennis pushed them out.

"Uncle Dennis, who was that?"

"Some friends from the apartment upstairs. They brought me some brownies."

Jacob liked brownies. "Can we have some?"

"I think you've had enough dessert tonight."

But he would have liked to taste the brownies. And after so much had been freely offered him, the denial came as a shock. But Jacob wouldn't have called for his parents to come get him because of feeling out of place. Something serious must have happened to Melody.

No one spoke of the events in North Carolina, and as far as Jacob knew, life had returned to normal.

One morning, the first week of sixth grade, Jacob and Melody were in the kitchen. Jacob was at the stove warming toast. Rose was splayed out on the floor in the Florida room. She was halfheartedly exercising in her pink babydoll nightie, not wanting to be bothered. She flipped through pages of an exercise book, one leg in the air, the other extended across the floor; scissors with pubic hair.

Melody was reaching for the refrigerator handle, which was near the stove.

"Be careful not to touch; it'll burn you," Jacob said.

"Jacob Murtaugh, I heard you," Rose screamed as she launched from scissors to standing, then stomping from the Florida room, around the dining room, into the kitchen. "Tell me what you just said to her."

"I told her not to touch the stove." Jacob already had tears in his eyes. Melody was sitting at the table pouring milk into a bowl of cereal. She didn't look up at him.

"You are lying, Jacob. You told her to *touch* the stove," said Rose.

"No, Mommy, I said not to touch it."

Rose slapped Jacob on the side of his head. "You're a liar. And since you wanted to burn your sister, I'm going to burn you. Touch that burner." The coil glowed red.

"No, Mommy. Please believe me. I didn't say that."

"I heard you. Touch it or I'll make you touch it. And it'll be worse if I have to do it."

"Mommy please no. Listen—" Rose grabbed his hand and pressed it onto the coil, holding it while she counted.

"One...Two...Three." She released Jacob's hand.

Screaming, he ran to the kitchen sink and stuck the searing flesh of his palm under the cold water.

"That's how I feel when you lie to me, Jacob. It burns my heart."

Their eyes met for a minute; Jacob did not reply. For he had nothing to say but felt something pass from himself to her as the water ran over his fingers and down his wrist. It was anger, it was hatred, it was overwhelming detachment, Rose knew, that made Jacob stare vacantly. You'll not hurt me again, he seemed to be saying. The feeling emboldened him. It enlarged him. None of her little snuggles, or promises, or matronly platitudes snuffed out his mind. Now the vigor of clarity and strength roused him; he would not be choked back. Walking past Rose, he shook his head. Melody never looked up from her cereal.

All Rose had in mind was to protect her daughter. She had watched a change come over Melody since she brought her back from North Carolina. Mama said she just got homesick, but Rose knew there was more to it. There was a suffocating air about it all, reminding Rose of being a little girl in her bedroom, alone with Klaus; of the tractor that ran her over on his farm; of the well she fell into as he left her; of memories just below the ground, stinking of formaldehyde and rot.

This is why she had to react so severely; to prove she would do anything to keep a man from hurting Melody. Because of her outrage, Rose knew she hadn't failed her daughter.

She went to Jacob, who was in the bathroom smearing ointment on his hand. "You'll not mention this to your father. If he finds out you made me do this to you, I'll beat you with the buckle-end of the belt again. Do you hear me?"

"Yes, Mommy."

"Now you go apologize to your sister."

Jacob walked down the hall toward the kitchen, as if he were in chains heading to the electric chair. His hand stung and throbbed. He looked at Melody. She glanced up at him in a way that made him hope she would say something to Rose; something to fix it all, so he wouldn't have to apologize.

"Are you going to say it?" Melody asked him.

"I didn't want you to hurt yourself. I'm sorry."

That summer, Jacob joined the Boy Scouts. His troop was scheduled to go on a day-long retreat at a lodge. The boys were to hike, canoe, fish, swim, build a campfire, and cook dinner. It was Jacob's first outing without his family (besides the usual field trips at school), and he did not want to swim; not because he couldn't—Rose and Edwin arranged swimming lessons when he was three-years-old—but because he did not want to change his clothes in front of the other boys.

"The Scout Master said everyone is swimming," snapped Rose.

"I don't want to, Mommy. I want to hike with David on the trails and look for turtles."

"You're going to participate, Jacob. Anyway, you'll earn the Water Safety badge. And why do you have such a problem changing clothes in front of other kids? It's not normal."

"I get uncomfortable," said Jacob, backing away from her. She jerked his red bathing suit out of his drawer and threw it at him.

"You're taking a bathing suit, and I'm packing a plastic bag for your wet clothes. You better have wet clothes, Jacob."

Jacob didn't change his clothes, and he didn't swim. He told the Cub Master his stomach hurt; he sat inside the lodge; he read a book.

Edwin, Rose, and Melody picked him up in the evening. Rose wanted a rundown of the day's activities.

"I found a painted turtle. I named him Lucky," said Jacob.

"Did you swim?" Rose asked. She had the ability to turn a conversation into an interrogation with the raising of an eyebrow. Jacob looked up at the rear-view mirror to try and catch his father's glance, to plead for help, but Edwin kept his eyes on the road.

If he told the truth, she would beat him. If he lied,

and she found out, she would beat him. But there was a chance she wouldn't catch him in the lie (he thought).

"Yes, I swam for a little bit. The water was really cold."

"You don't look wet at all," Rose said. She leaned over the front seat and flicked his cap from his head. "Your hair is dry as dirt."

"We swam in the morning, Mommy."

"Give me your bag." Jacob clutched the bag tighter. "Give me the bag, Jacob." Edwin squinted and leaned forward, pretending to search the road for danger.

Rose grabbed Jacob's bag and pulled out his bathing suit. It occurred to him then, he should have run his bathing suit under a faucet and put it back in the plastic bag. But there it was, as clean and dry as when she had taken it out of his drawer.

"You lied, Jacob. You didn't swim. What is wrong with you?"

"He just gets embarrassed, Rose. Calm down."

"You stay out of this, Edwin. You don't have to deal with him day in, day out." She turned back to Jacob with such severity. "When we get home Jacob, I'm going to spank you. But you've got to learn your lesson. Take off all of your clothes right now."

"Rose, stop it," pleaded Edwin weakly. Jacob stripped down to his underwear.

"Take those off, too. You're going to walk down the street, up our driveway, and into our house buck-naked. Maybe then you'll get over this."

Jacob was crying. Would there be neighbors out at this hour? Other cars? Edwin protested a few more times until Rose began shrieking for him to pull over. Melody watched in silence, relieved none of this had anything to

92

do with her.

Edwin stopped the car a good distance down the street from their house. Rose got out and opened Jacob's door. "Take off that underwear." Jacob did. His face was wet from tears, and his hands shook in terror. Rose pulled him out of the car and slammed his door. "Now, walk home."

His family drove off. The poorly paved road scraped his feet as he tried to run. The closer he came to the house, the sooner the beating would follow. But someone might see if he slowed down. He ran as quickly as he could toward the inevitable.

Jacob and Shawn wandered on their bikes through the fields behind their subdivision. Past the dirt roads and barb-wire fences, they came to a large wooden barn. The evening's last shard of sunlight painted a corner of the building basketball-orange. Shawn jumped off his bike and headed for the barn door; he motioned for Jacob to follow. Inside, the smell of hay, brown and dry, weighted the air with dust. Golden flecks drifted in the blue-gray light, like snowfall in reverse.

"This is the perfect place to grill our dogs," said Shawn. "You're the Boy Scout, start us a fire."

Jacob brought in the twigs he had gathered and lit them. Shawn threw on dried hay. Soon, the orange and yellow flames rose higher. Pulling together two bails, the boys made seats next to each other near the fire. They grilled their hot dogs and watched the crease in the lavender sky fold into the purple of twilight.

After they ate, Shawn jumped on top of Jacob and pinned his hands to the ground. His touch sent a current through Jacob's body. It jolted like a static shock from rubbing socks on the carpet and touching metal. The tingling warmed until Jacob didn't feel Shawn's hands, but he felt the place where Shawn was touching.

These are my hands, the way they feel to him.

"You make a pretty good fire," said Shawn. His green eyes drifted closer to Jacob's face. Jacob lifted his head slightly and parted his lips.

Shawn snatched a handful of hay and spread it over Jacob's hair. "We should put out this fire and get going."

"The proper way to put out a fire is to cover it up with dirt," said Jacob.

"I know that, and I'm not even a Boy Scout."

They walked their bikes through the brush debating whether Metallica or Iron Maiden played heavier metal. When they reached the outskirts of the subdivision, Shawn hopped on his bike and yelled, "Race ya!"

Jacob was struck by Shawn's power. He wanted Shawn to win.

When Jacob finally came around the bend near his house, he saw Shawn stopped in the middle of the street. Two police cars sat in Jacob's driveway.

"I'll come in with you," said Shawn. "To find out what's going on."

"No, you go on home. I'll call you."

The fire had started near the boys' impromptu fire pit. The barn, stacked with bails of hay, burned to the ground.

"The damage is over one hundred thousand dollars," said the officer. "What were you boys doing in there?" Jacob told him everything through tears, his voice trembling.

The police officer called the barn owner who said he wouldn't press charges, considering he knew the boys' parents, and that they really didn't intend any harm. In private, the officer told Jacob's parents the barn was falling apart anyway, and the hay wasn't going to be used. But he thought a Boy Scout should know better than to start a fire in the middle of a hay barn.

He cautioned: "No amount of dirt can cover up every ember." ✣

CHAPTER VIII

Genie In A Lamp

Jacob endured his punishments for starting the fire. Rose intended on spanking him (spanking was always her first remedy), but Edwin persuaded her to ground him from television and forbid him to play with Shawn for three weeks. She also took his candles away indefinitely, which Jacob protested.

Life hobbled along for Jacob as when one suffers a broken leg: moving forward is painful at first; one is aware of every step. In time, he was on the mend and adjusted to Rose's restrictions. His parents didn't harp on him about the barn. They seemed preoccupied with issues at the furniture store. Late one night, Jacob overheard them arguing about having to repay Faith the remainder of her loan; the store wasn't making enough to bring Paul on as a partner. There was talk of selling the store.

Every afternoon while he couldn't see Shawn, Jacob stepped off the bus, kissed Jean Ann's cheek, sucked down a glass of cold milk, and cut a hunk of cheese for the bike ride.

"I'm going over to Wayne's house. Mom always lets me."

"Have you done your homework?" asked Jean Ann.

"Wayne will help me with it," said Jacob on the way out the door.

An interior designer for Edwin at the furniture store, Wayne was in his thirties and owned a house at the end of the street. The Mid-Century Modern architecture that prevailed upon every home in Rolling Green had been dispensed with, as Wayne's house underwent reconstructive surgery. Gray wooden slats and slick black shingles replaced the painted white brick and sandpaper-like roof. Pillars were disposed of, and an open porch was installed with a water feature and natural foliage. In the back, Wayne had a gray wooden deck built for the pool. Large Romanesque vases overstuffed with prickly grasses and palms concealed the surround-sound speakers and mood lighting. There was always music playing.

Jacob knocked on the back door.

No answer.

He let himself in. "Wayne, it's Jacob."

"In the hallway, hon."

"What are you doing on the floor?" Wayne was sitting on the charcoal-gray carpet in front of a walk-in closet in the hallway. He had removed photographs from their frames and scattered them across the floor. His eyes were puffy and red.

"Why do you have these pictures of you and Guy all over the place?"

"Guy is moving out, Jacob. Do you know what

that means?"

"He's moving away someplace?"

"Sort of. Hasn't your mother told you anything?" Wayne had arranged the photos in some kind of order, then shuffled them like a deck of cards.

"About what?"

Jacob became conscious of Wayne's stare. One eyebrow was raised, quizzically, as if he were mocking Jacob's naiveté, but at the same time Wayne was urging him, *Go ahead, ask me anything you want. Please.*

"She said she went dancing in Tampa with you last week. She didn't come back until morning. I had to fix me and Melody breakfast because she didn't wake up in time to get us ready for school."

Wayne shook his head. He wondered what it was like to be Rose's son, to live with her scrutiny and severity. He wondered if she knew what kind of boy she was raising—a boy who was a slave to her every need, who believed if he didn't satisfy his mother's every whim she would wither and die.

Wayne was skinny, tan, and tall. He had hazel-green eyes, a trim beard, and a Louisiana drawl. Jacob liked to watch him move, graceful and birdlike.

"What's that?" Jacob pointed to a brass genie lamp.

"It's an incense burner."

"I love incense."

"You also like to burn barns down, I hear," said Wayne. "But I don't have it just for the incense, darlin'."

"Why else do you have it?"

Wayne put his forefinger and thumb together and brought it to his mouth. He drew in a deep breath and held it, then waved the air with his hand as he blew out. Jacob laughed.

"Oh, I get it. I've never done that before."

"You probably will one day. Would ya like to have the lamp?"

Jacob picked it up and rubbed it. "Yeah, I'd love it, as long as I can have the genie too."

"Of course you can, hon. Just don't go rubbin' it too much. And for God sakes, don't tell your mother I gave it to you. And don't burn your house down, either. Take some incense." Wayne collected the photographs from the floor. "Did your friend get in trouble too?"

"Yeah, we can't see each other for three weeks."

"So bring him over here. I won't tell."

"Really? I'll see if he wants to come swimming."

"As long as you don't drown each other. At least you won't be burning anything down."

"Got anything to eat?" asked Jacob.

"Let's go to the kitchen. I'll make dinner, but you have to help. A boy your age needs to learn how to cook."

Wayne brought out a whole chicken from the refrigerator. Digging and scraping into its body cavity, he removed the guts.

"Disgusting. You don't wear gloves for that?" Jacob screwed his face up.

"Honey, these are gonna be good eatin'. Now start choppin' the carrots. There's a knife in that drawer."

Wayne washed and dried the neck and shook it in Jacob's face.

"What's that make you think of?"

"A dick," said Jacob, cringing with self-consciousness.

"Boys have such dirty minds," said Wayne, winking. "Make those slices thinner."

"Wayne, kids at school call me faggot."

"Well, if that's what you are, that's what you are. There's nothing wrong with it."

It was as easy as an honest exchange between two people cleaning chicken and cutting vegetables with patchouli incense and disco music drifting through the kitchen; it was innocent and natural for each to drop the veil of everyday charades; for each to allow a shard of light to wedge itself into their sordid closets of secrets, and declare everything in them human and acceptable.

From his bed that night, Jacob wondered if Wayne could be his teacher. Could he show him how to soar, to slip barriers, to dive and to rise above the clouds?

Jacob felt the sheets beneath him. *This is the spot where Shawn lay*, Jacob remembered.

The green-glowing cross on his wall rebuked him. Outside he saw the yellow security light had been triggered. Must be a cat. The face of Jesus was now in half shadow. He wished for the darkness. He turned away from the Lord's stare and closed his eyes. The tastes and smells of his friend were a blink away.

Wayne's acceptance was unbearable. It burned and festered as the transfigured Christ watched Jacob commit lecherous acts beneath the sheets.

"Follow me," Jesus beckoned, with a face contorted in pain. "Cast your net on the right side, and you will find me." Jesus' words blazed red in Jacob's mind as the sheet stopped moving up and down.

The right side is always better.
Click teeth. Nod.
Everything is okay.

It was a Friday, cleaning day for Rose. Jacob was dusting his bookshelf when she came into his room for an inspection.

"Where did you get this incense burner?" demanded Rose.

"Wayne gave it to me."

"Sit down, Jacob. Jean Ann told me you've been going to Wayne's every day after school."

"Yes, ma'am he's been helping me with my homework."

"Jacob, Wayne is gay. Do you know what that means?" Jacob began to cry.

"No, Mommy."

"Jacob, tell me the truth. I always know when you're lying."

"What does it mean?" he asked her. He remembered the chicken neck and the black and white photo of Guy standing behind Wayne with his arms wrapped around his neck.

"It's when two men act like they love each other and do nasty things. It's against the Bible. Now answer me. Are you gay?"

"I'm not like that. Why would you even think I am?"

"The way you hold your hand, the way you talk; you're spending all your time at Wayne's house alone. It's not natural. I'm concerned Jacob; you are the only one who can carry on the Murtaugh name. Do you understand?"

Jacob thought for a moment, his face clouded with resentment, his mind twisted into a whorl where he looked out at Rose like some emperor who, finding his public gathered in his courtyard, glares from his throne and rejects their protestations and requests.

But obedience prevailed. He bowed his head shamefully and said, "Yes, I understand."

"Don't bring this up to your father, and give me all the incense sticks. From now on you can only go to Wayne's when I'm with you. You need to spend time with friends your own age. A girlfriend would be nice."

Jacob struggled to ask Jesus for forgiveness; compounding his sins every night. "Please don't let me be like Wayne," he prayed before he thought about the boys in the shower during dress-out. He blanked Jesus out as he wiped himself, then asked in vain for Christ's help. To truly be forgiven, he had to repent, which meant he had to want to change himself, but he didn't know how or who to turn to.

After a few weeks, the pray-sin-pray ritual became rote. Some nights Jacob was nearly asleep as he threw the tissue in the trash. The next morning he feared he had not asked the Savior to spare him, so he prayed again, and again, and again: "Please don't let me be gay." Had he asked properly with focus? He'd better pray it again to get it right.

Click teeth, nod, Jesus forgives all.

The shiny genie lamp caught his attention mid-prayer; he wondered if anyone was listening.

"Are we going to your house or mine?" asked Shawn on the bus ride home from school.

"Let's go to mine," said Jacob.

Jean Ann's truck wasn't in the driveway. Jacob found the house key under the mat.

"There's a note," said Jacob. "Jean Ann and Melody went into town to get groceries."

"You know what that means!" Shawn threw his school bag on the floor.

"What are we going to do? We prolly have an hour." Jacob hoped Shawn would head to the bedroom.

"Let's play a practical joke on them," said Shawn. "We can hide and jump out when they come in."

"Good idea. But I've got an even better one. Let's make the house look like someone broke in and kidnapped us."

"Man, that's sick. How?"

"I have a leather glove. I'll stuff it with cotton and fill it with so much ketchup it'll ooze out. Then we'll put a knife in the bloody hand and set it by the door. You make a ketchup blob trail around it."

"Okay, then we'll turn some chairs over to look like there was a struggle. When your nanny and sister get home, they'll freak out."

"When we hear one of them scream, we'll jump out and scare them," said Jacob.

The boys got to work on their plan. Jacob took care to find a spot to place the glove plainly in view. He stepped into the garage and opened the door a few times to check the angle. The vision twisted his intent from fun to fury; a wildness came over him as he darted from room to room to find the next piece of the scene to unsettle.

Curtains spread open unevenly. The house was dark. Water ran in the kitchen sink. The garage door was cracked open.

Everything was ready.

The boys heard Jean Ann's diesel truck pull up the drive. They shared a quick, frenzied glance and ducked their heads behind an overturned sofa.

"Jean Ann the door is open," said Melody, backing away. Jean Ann peeked through the crack and immediately closed the door. The boys heard them running from the house. When the phone rang, Jacob answered.

"Jacob, this is Jean Ann. Are you okay?"

"Yes, ma'am. Shawn and I were just playing a joke."

"It's not funny. You two stay where you are."

Jacob told Shawn to run home. He was out the back door and up the hill before Jean Ann walked in.

"I was about to call the police." Jean Ann's jowls shook with violence. "You scared us."

A crooked smile tried to pry itself free as fear bloomed in Melody's face. "I thought you were dead, Bubba."

"Your sister was crying hysterically." Jean Ann's hands wrapped around Melody's head like blinders.

Jacob couldn't see any tears. Her eyes weren't red.

"Go outside and find a switch, Jacob."

"Yes, ma'am."

"And it better be a long one, and it better not break."

Jacob picked through the dried twigs in the bramble on top of the hill behind the house. They were too brittle. He tore a long, wiry branch from the maple tree.

Jean Ann swatted his bare legs hard enough to leave welts.

Jacob waited in his bedroom the rest of the afternoon

for his parents to come home from the furniture store. Jean Ann told them everything. Edwin gave him a lecture then comforted Melody. Rose told Jacob he must have a mental illness and would need counseling. She said he was lucky Jean Ann didn't call the cops, and he was double lucky she was still willing to work for them.

Rose opened Edwin's closet door. Jacob heard a belt buckle clang against its siblings as she withdrew it from the bunch. Edwin softly read Melody a nighttime story, stroking her hair.

"Go into the bathroom and pull down your pants," said Rose.

"Mommy, please don't. At least let me keep my pants up."

Rose pushed Jacob to the floor and whipped his back with the belt buckle. The square metal clipped his wrist and knees as Jacob flailed in self-defense.

"I said take your pants down."

Jacob did. She lashed him several more times down his legs, his rear-end, and back. She struck hard, like when she beat dust out of the carpets hanging on the clothesline.

"Get on your pajamas and go to bed. No supper. You're going to see Pastor MacDonald tomorrow."

Jacob looked at Jesus on the wall. The glow-in-the-dark cross, chimerical and toy-like, mocked him.

Jacob wept. ❧

CHAPTER IX

Perfect Submission

Pastor MacDonald liked Jacob to serve as an acolyte on Sunday mornings. Other boys threw their cassocks over their clothes at the last minute, grabbed the candle lighter, and took their seats in the chancel. Jacob arrived early, polished the bell snuffer, made sure the bookmarks were set for the Celebrant, organized the bulletins in the Narthex, all while having donned his pressed cassock, tied with the perfect cincture. Jacob was devoted to Christ, that MacDonald recognized, but he hoped in some small way Jacob understood he was also serving the pastor.

Mrs. MacDonald greeted Jacob and Rose at the parsonage wearing a lime-green polyester skirt with a matching jacket and a striped sherbet blouse accented with a pearl necklace. The style screamed pastor's wife, which made Jacob feel comfortable.

Rose pursed her lips and tried to hold a smile on her

109

face. Slipping, losing her hold presently, her expression fell, revealing another woman beneath. But here she must come, so Jacob could get better. She had taken stock; the embarrassment she would suffer was worth the risk, for she didn't know how to help him, couldn't begin to understand his behavior. Face buttressed, she stepped into the parsonage.

"Pastor will see you in his study," said Mrs. MacDonald. "Follow me if you don't mind."

If we don't mind, thought Jacob. He minded. He liked Pastor MacDonald, but he didn't want to tell him what he'd done; to divulge the fake blood, the glove, the knife; and what had Rose already told him? Had she said anything about Shawn? How she thought he was a bad influence? Was she half-baked enough to tell pastor about her friend Wayne? Had she mentioned their all-night dancing trips to Tampa? About her notes to Jacob left on the kitchen counter: "Mommy is too tired again. Long night." And could he take out the cereal and pour milk for Melody while she slept? Well, that was the solution! He'd had enough of her leaving him to go party with Wayne, grounding him from seeing his best friend, putting the pressure on him to take care of his sister, and get himself to school. Besides, he and Shawn were only letting off steam. He decided to tell Pastor MacDonald about the beating.

"I want to talk to the boy alone, Rose," said pastor MacDonald.

"What time should I come back and get him?"

"I'll drive him home."

"Thank you very much, Pastor."

Jacob didn't like the idea of an open-ended appointment. How long would he have to talk about all of this? What if he was ready to leave? He looked at his mother and gave her his best pleading face. She ignored him.

Jacob was alone with Pastor MacDonald, which was like being alone with God. He looked around the office. There were books from floor to ceiling behind the man, framing him in authority. His high-back, blood-brown leather chair squeaked when he adjusted his large frame. His round, maroon face nearly matched the upholstery. The room was dim, cast in marine hues like the blue between the sea and sky. The afternoon sun sifted through thick, blue cotton curtains.

"You're a very obedient boy, Jacob. But it seems you've upset your mother. Why don't you tell me your version of what happened." Leaning forward, MacDonald patted Jacob's knee. His meaty palm covered it entirely. He had never touched Jacob before. As Jacob recounted the facts from the beginning, the pastor let his hand settle, warming Jacob's knee, then like a worm, it inched up his thigh.

MacDonald interrupted him when he came to the part about the notes on the counter.

"You say they went out dancing, this Wayne and your mother?" MacDonald wheeled his mammoth chair closer to Jacob.

"Yes, sir. She left me a note the morning after."

"And when did that all start?"

"About a month before the prank."

"I see. It's all terribly interesting. And you say this

Wayne is also a friend of yours?"

"Well, yes, sir. But he's really my mom's friend. Actually, he works at the furniture store my mom and dad own."

"And this buddy of yours, Shawn. Tell me about him."

Jacob talked about how he and Shawn met. How at first he had to pretend not to know him until Shawn decided Jacob was cool.

"Now he always picks me to be on his teams at recess. And we sit together at lunch. I even gave him a ring, a best friend ring. I have one too. See?"

"He must mean an awful lot to you, Jacob."

"I was angry when my mom wouldn't let me see him."

"Angry enough to want to kill someone?"

"No way. That's extreme."

"Then why such a gory prank?" asked MacDonald.

"We wanted to scare my sister and freak out Jean Ann."

"But the two of you burned a barn down, Jacob. Wasn't that on purpose too?"

"No. Is that what she told you? It's not true. That was an accident, and it was all my fault, not Shawn's. Pastor, she's lying. She's making up lies because she's doing wrong. She's going out and getting into all kinds of trouble. And then—" Jacob stopped to consider how MacDonald would conceive of what he would say next. How does one rat out his mother to a man of God? How does a son explain that he's terrified of the woman who gave birth to him?

But the chance to get back at her for lying about Shawn pushed the words out of Jacob's mouth. "She beat the hell out of me with my father's belt, Pastor. And my dad didn't even stop her!"

MacDonald's silver bifocals slid down his greasy nose as he raised his shaggy eyebrows.

"Show me," MacDonald said.

"It's just marks up and down my back, Pastor. Bruises and welts. She's done it since I was a kid."

"I'm so sorry, Jacob. Abuse like that is never okay, but I need to see the bruises. Take off your clothes, down to your underwear." He got up off the high-back chair and walked to the pocket door to lock it. "It's just us. No one will come in."

Until MacDonald locked the door, Jacob had felt hope; he had hoped MacDonald was listening to him and could hear the insanity in his family; he had hoped the pastor might be the one to reach his large, strong hand down into Jacob's messy life and pull him out, as God did for Moses and the Israelites when they were rescued from Pharaoh and brought out of Egypt into the Promised Land; he had hoped MacDonald could be his teacher, bedecked in black, his white squared collar beneath his neck—a shining beacon of knowledge and comfort.

Jacob stood in front of Pastor MacDonald, now seated in his office chair. MacDonald removed his clergy collar and threw it on the desk. His breathing was like a horse brought to stable after a race.

Take off your clothes, he had said. It sounded like, "Fetch the candle lighter," or "Hand me the hymnal." Jacob pulled off his shirt and jeans. MacDonald ran his hand over Jacob's back, pausing at the first bruise.

Set out the hymnal for the service.

"She did this?" he asked. Jacob nodded, his body

frozen, his mind cemented behind the padded place deep past his eyes.

God is not here, boomed The Voice in his head.

Set out the host for the congregants.

MacDonald's hand moved past the band of his underwear towards his buttocks.

Pour the wine.

"Did she hit you here, too?" Jacob nodded in reply.

Don't snuff out the candles yet.

"I'm going to need to take some pictures. For evidence." He let his hand expand the waistline and reached around the front to cup Jacob's privates. He said nothing. He didn't look at Jacob. He only felt Jacob grow in his clutch.

Lamb of God, you take away the sin of the world. Have mercy upon us.

Jacob counted the flashes from the camera.

"Turn and face the window," MacDonald told him.

Flash.

He knelt behind Jacob, looking; touching; whispering. White-Blue lights filled the room like fireworks. "Face me," he said.

Flash.

Jacob had never heard an adult order him to do something in a way that sounded like he was begging.

Flash.

MacDonald put his warm lips around Jacob. At first, he swelled sliding in and out of Pastor MacDonald's plump mouth; he gasped watching this man on his knees; he trembled as this servant of God served him as Jacob had done so often during the Eucharist. Jacob placed his hands on MacDonald's bald spot.

May He make His face shine upon you.

And then it was over. MacDonald suckled like a hungry piglet. Jacob was sickened by the man's lust. And sickened because he knew Jesus couldn't love him for what he was doing. Sickened for knowing his parents would hate him. Sickened for wishing it was Shawn instead.

"I want to go home," he shoved MacDonald off him and got dressed. "We're not doing this again."

"Of course I'll take you home, Jacob."

Pastor MacDonald needed to speak with Rose. Edwin was still at the store. She put dinner on the back-burner and sat down next to Pastor MacDonald in the living room.

"Jacob, you can go to your room," she said.

After he left, MacDonald folded his hands and leaned forward. "Your boy is very disturbed, Rose. He needs help; far more than I can provide. He's angry about many things; I think the entire family is in need of professional counseling. In fact, I feel there's a lot of anger happening behind the scenes."

"Yes, Pastor, we're under a lot of stress financially."

"Consider yourself lucky for catching the warning signs early. Look through the Yellow Pages and find a good counselor. He's a good boy. It'd be a shame to lose him to society's ills. Drugs and crime are on the rise. He's on the crux of becoming a teenager; falling in with the wrong crowd could throw him off track for years."

"Yes, sir. Edwin and I will see what we can do. Thank you for taking up your afternoon with him."

"It was my pleasure. Let's say a prayer before I leave,

shall we?"

Pastor MacDonald prayed that Christ would protect Jacob from all danger and harm. That through Christ, God should show mercy on the Murtaugh family and sustain them by His grace. It was a long prayer. Rose peeked through squinted eyes.

MacDonald fervently shook his folded hands and nodded his cherry face and spit through his fat, wet lips. Sweat beaded on his forehead where his hairline was receding. He wasn't the fiery Baptist preachers she grew up with (or sometimes still liked to watch on Sunday mornings when she didn't feel like going to church), but she figured he meant well.

She uttered a loud, "Amen," hoping God would at least help and not blame her for screwing up Jacob, which she had surely done, somehow. ❧

CHAPTER X

Models of the World

Edwin finished taking down the Labor Day sale signs in the window. He told Wayne to go home, he and Rose would finish cleaning the store. He needed to say things to her in private. Wayne would take Rose's side; inject opinions Edwin didn't need. For this was his business, his future, and it was failing.

All the years, all the events, all the sales, all the advertisements, all the parties, all the success, and he could not bring Paul down from New York because of Rose; because she wasn't careful with their money. She wanted the clothes, the latest model Buick, the trips to Tampa to shop, to dance, to go out to eat, the redecoration of the house, the vacations; all of it took her away from Pierceville (she called it "Dodge City"). The place was a constant reminder of her parents' home; no matter what Edwin did, he could never take her far enough away from there. Only Wayne seemed to bring her a brief reprieve,, but then his life was one fantasy after another.

"Why did you send Wayne home? We need help cleaning, and he needs the pay. I've been on my feet all day, and my back is killing me."

"You sit and rest. Pick a recliner. There's a whole row that didn't sell. I need to talk to you."

She knew what he was going to say. He wanted to let Wayne go and some of the delivery men, too. Edwin wasn't shrewd like she was. She would work them up until the very end. He was gracious, like his mother, and full of pride. He would want to spare the most loyal from seeing the whole thing flounder.

"What are we going to do if we sell, Edwin? How much will we make and what can we keep after we pay Faith back on the loan?"

"We would have a small nest egg to live on for a while if we're careful." Edwin made sure to look at her when he said, "careful." "And I think this could be our chance to get out of here. We could sell the house and move closer to Tampa."

"I'd like that. It's closer to Mama and Daddy. We could live in a suburb. Would we make enough from the sale of this house to build another?"

"I think so. We have to be careful." Edwin's tone emphasized "careful," but he didn't look at her.

"Don't you lecture me about being careful, Eddie." Rose's mind had flown off the handle before her mouth opened. "Why are you accusing me? You're just as bad as I am. You tell me you and Jim are going out on those repo runs then you end up in some bar drinking yourselves silly. And all the golf games on Sundays, the new television sets and radios for your sports games, the toys you buy for the kids instead of giving them your time, because all you really want to do is—" She couldn't say the rest. She remembered the magazines of nude men Jacob found in Edwin's golf bag. Naked men. Homosexual men. "I just want this family to be happy. For the kids to be happy," she said. She took the broom and began to sweep the floor. "Let's sell it all."

Lying across the bed in Jacob's room, Shawn and Jacob listened to cassette tapes. Over the summer, Jacob saved some of his lawn-mowing money and bought the Synchronicity album by The Police. The boys were scribing the words to "Every Breath You Take," writing down a phrase, rewinding the tape, pressing their ears close to the speaker, then hitting play again.

"He's saying, 'I've been lost without a race,'" insisted Shawn.

"That doesn't even make sense," said Jacob, "Play it again."

Jacob heard sounds from outside—a shrill noise like a bird or a rabbit, the futile protests, the shock, the dismay of being caught in a death-bite. Shawn turned down the music. Melody was screaming.

"Shit, something's going on," said Shawn.

They ran out to find Shawn's nine-year-old brother and Melody standing red-faced, nearly in a brawl.

"I told him to stop, but he wouldn't," said Melody.

"What did you do, Joey?" Shawn shoved him away from Melody.

Melody's yellow dress was smudged with dirt, the bow hung down like spaghetti strings, and her panties shackled her ankles.

"She said we could play like we were making babies," said Joey.

"Get your panties back on, Melody, and go inside." Jacob clenched his hand, thinking of the burn from the oven. Would he be blamed for this, too?

"I better get him home. You gonna tell your parents?" asked Shawn.

"I don't know. Probably. You?"

"Yeah, I guess so."

Rose broke down. She knew the world was a wicked place, teaming with sexual perverts, but she never thought a young boy would assault her daughter in her backyard. And to think, Melody let him! What had possessed her to let a boy pull his pants down and touch her with his penis? And where was Jacob? What was he doing instead of watching his sister? Rose recalled the advice Pastor MacDonald gave her. They needed counseling. But where? She phoned her friend Jacqueline Gregory from the church choir. She had used a counselor before.

"We have to do something, Jacqueline. All this sex stuff with Melody, and the violence with Jacob. I'm losing control of my family, and I don't know where to turn. Even Pastor MacDonald said it needs to be a professional."

"I know of a wonderful woman. You have to call her. But you should know, she's not a Christian. She's involved in the Humanistic Psychology movement, but she's really good, Rose. She helped my family and me. She saved us."

"What kind of therapy is that?"

"It treats the whole person. It's not like where they lay you down on a couch, scribble a bunch of notes while you chatter away, and then throw medicine at you. I really think Jacob will respond." Rose took down the number. She read it several times. The clinic was in Tampa. "Visualize Greatness," she read out loud. She ran her finger across the counselor's name: Rue Pedersen.

Needing time to get the family's story together, Rose wanted to put off calling until the next day. She couldn't just tell it like it was, what with Jacob terrorizing Jean Ann with a bloody glove and a knife, and Melody pulling her skirt up for boys in the neighborhood. Or could she? Maybe these problems were just what a Humanistic counselor could deal with. She picked up the phone and dialed the number.

"Yes, I'd like to schedule an appointment with Rue Pedersen. Nothing until next month? But I think my daughter may have been molested. Please tell her that." Rose didn't know why she said it. Suddenly, Rue was on the line.

"My God, child, what on earth are you having to deal with. How are you holding up?"

Her raspy voice, the realness of her tone, made her sound as if she were in the very room with Rose. It was the kind of presence Rose wished Audrey had. She grabbed her stomach and held back the shrieks behind her tears.

"I don't know, Mrs. Pedersen. My family is falling apart."

"Can you bring the babies tomorrow evening. I'll stay late."

Jacob and Melody waited in the lobby while Edwin and Rose spoke with Rue. Jacob adjusted his glasses and tried to read the framed posters all around. He leaned forward (his nearsighted vision had begun to get worse) and saw a picture of a bean with big eyes and a smiling face. He made out the words, "You're a human doing, not a human bean." What did it mean? he wondered. What was the difference between a human that did things as opposed to a human that just was? He read another poster: "I'm ok—you're ok." Underneath that were three overlapping circles with the intersecting arcs shaded with blue. Inside each read, "Parent," "Adult," "Child."

All of this began to give him a feeling of freedom. Perhaps he could be a human who was okay. He thought of Jonathan Livingston Seagull and wondered if he might find a teacher behind that door.

Rue stuck her head into the lobby. "Children, please come." Her bright big blue eyes, small smiling mouth, and tiny nose gave her a childlike appearance. She also wasn't much taller than Jacob, not counting her altitudinous blonde bouffant hair.

She took Melody's hand but spoke to Jacob. "I hear you know my friend Jaqueline Gregory."

Yes, he knew her.

"And she gave you one of my favorite books."

"You've read Jonathan Livingston Seagull?"

Rue cackled. She put her hand on her heart and laughed some more. "I have, indeed, child. And I know how to fly."

Jacob wondered if she meant an airplane (his thoughts could be very literal at times), or did she know some secrets?

As the children came into Rue's office, they saw their parents on a large, off-white couch, one of them sitting at each end. They looked as if they'd been skewered in their positions. Rue handed Melody a doll and a few other playthings and told the children a story about a monster who had been let out of his cage by an evil witch who wanted to take over the village. The king and queen didn't know what to do, so they went to the edge of the forest where a wizard lived. The wizard knew a spell that could put the monster back in the cage. But there was just one problem. The wizard needed a special ingredient for her potion, and she just happened to be out.

"Do you know what that ingredient was?" Rue looked at Jacob, then Melody.

"Cinnamon?" asked Melody. Rue laughed from her belly. Her laugh bounced off the dimly lit cream walls of her office, like a fairy sprinkling its dust here and there. She reached into her purse and brought out a Benson & Hedges 100, lit it, toked and puffed out a white cloud—all in one orchestrated motion—and turned to Jacob. "What do you think was missing, love?"

"Courage," Jacob said.

"That wasn't what I was going to say, but Good God, that's a damn fine answer." Jacob had never heard an adult cuss on purpose in front of him before. He liked that she did.

"Melody, you've been really scared lately. And I know you are very close to your brother. And I think you've been afraid to say how scared you are." Melody's eyes locked onto Rue's. She hugged the doll and stopped

AKIVA HERSH

moving. "Love, it's all right for Jacob to know that he scared you. He needs to know about it, and you need to tell him. That way, things will feel better between you two. Will you do an experiment with me?"

"I guess," said Melody.

"I want you to pretend you have a magic hand. Will you put your hand out for me?" Rue demonstrated. "Put your hand out with your palm, this part, facing your brother."

Melody did.

"And for as long hold out your palm, Jacob has to move across the room away from you, until he's far enough away that you begin to feel safe again."

Melody held her little pink palm out like a traffic cop. From behind, half of her face peered at Jacob, stern as granite. She did look scared, thought Jacob. He looked at Rue; she smiled kindly as if to encourage him. He looked at his father; Edwin's body sat on the sofa, but his mind had gone. His face was as blank as a corpse. He looked at his mother; Rose's face seemed to have caved in, seemed to have drawn like a curtain. Her expression reminded him of when they watched horror movies. Her hands fidgeted. She pulled her jaws tight. Her eyes bulged; she sat still, without blinking.

"Jacob, slowly move away from Melody," said Rue.

Jacob scooted back on the carpet. Melody's hand didn't go down. In fact, she pushed her palm further toward him. Jacob scooted back a few feet more. Again, she pushed. Jacob stood and walked backward several steps until he was clear across the room. Melody lowered her hand and looked at Rue. She nodded her head.

"Jacob, take a seat where you are. How do you feel over there?"

"Sad," he said, but he really felt angry, for how could he tell Rue he was mad at Melody? Rue might say it was wrong to be mad; she might say his sister has every right to want him far away. Why was everybody making this all about Melody? All he did was make a stupid glove with some ketchup. Wasn't he going to get a chance to talk about Pastor MacDonald? No, he couldn't. *Melody means more to them than you do. Especially to your father.* The Voice confirmed Jacob's fear. Edwin always had favored her.

It was then Jacob felt sad, for himself and for Melody. Hadn't they been brought together to protect each other? Hadn't they laughed and played, inventing people to become and worlds to inhabit? Hadn't they comforted each other at night when the darkness came? Had Jacob failed her?

"What do you want here, Jacob?" asked Rue.

"I don't want Melody to be afraid of me anymore."

"I get that, love. So what is it you *do* want?"

"I want us to be safe," he said.

Rue worked at creating a space for the siblings to close the distance and reestablish the connection between them. Before they left, she wanted Melody to be able to give Jacob safe signals for when she felt threatened and comfort signals for when she wanted him close. Then Jacob was sent out of the room, back to the lobby. What did they have to talk about that was worse than bloody gloves and knives? Jacob wanted to know.

Melody put down the doll and stood in front of Rue

sitting in her antique gold chenille armchair that seemed to snuggle her like a large person.

"Would you like to crawl in my lap, love?"

Melody answered her by climbing into the chair.

"Now what have you to say to your mommy and daddy?"

Now is the time to tell them, thought Melody. Maybe because Jacob isn't here, or because Rue is. She thought about Boo Boo (her name for Klaus Ramburg), which gave way to a feeling, to a knowing, that what she had to say would slow her mother down, maybe for good. For all the running, the dance lessons, the parties; the weekend-long visits where she and Jacob were left with Jean Ann and her family so Mommy and Daddy could go away together; the trips to Disney, the vacations, this would make her stop.

"Boo Boo touched my pee-pee."

Rose bit her finger, then covered her face and began to bawl.

"Rose. Rose, look at me," said Rue.

"Yes, ma'am?"

"Look at your daughter. She isn't done yet. Take a deep breath and listen. Edwin, you can hold Rose's hand, if that's all right." He reached out his hand, and she took it.

"Boo Boo touched your pee-pee? Where did this happen?" asked Rue.

"At their house, in the blue bedroom, when me and Jacob were sleeping. And in the cowshed. And in North Carolina."

"So he's been doing this a long time," Rue said.

"That bastard," said Edwin, grimacing, pounding his fist, shaking his head. The corpse had resurrected. "Rose, you better be glad we don't own a gun or—"

"Oh, shut up, Edwin, you don't have the balls to—"

"People, there's a child here, and this is about her." Rue held her finger in the air as a warning. She looked into Melody's face and stroked her cheek with that finger. "Melody, you're doing just fine. Your parents are scared and hurt for you. That's perfectly okay. Tell us the rest."

Through the lobby door, Jacob heard his mother sobbing. His stomach sank. Had Carol Alice and Lena told Melody what they'd done? Was she ratting on him? Making up lies? Did she suspect something was going on with him and Shawn?

"He said he'd kill Ruby if I told." Melody hid her face into Rue's bosom.

"Who is Ruby?" Rue asked.

"She's our poodle," said Rose, grasping her throat as if to choke herself, wishing to choke her father.

"Let the child speak, Rose," said Rue. "We need to hear her tell it."

"I wanted him to stop but—"

Melody had no more words. Rue cradled her and whispered love and acceptance over her wounds like a salve.

Finally, Jacob's family came out to the lobby. Rose told him to go in to speak to Rue by himself.

He sat down in a leather swivel chair facing her. He ran his feet back and forth over the camelhair throw rug.

"Jacob, I'm going to have to ask you to stop doing that. It's genuine camelhair, and your shoes could ruin the rug."

Jacob must've looked severely scolded, for Rue chuckled, leaned forward and said, "Jacob, there's not a thing wrong with you. I like you very much. It's perfectly okay to ask someone to stop doing something you don't like, and it doesn't mean you are rejecting the person."

What an insight! Yes, a teacher, thought Jacob. For Rue had demonstrated a power he had not known one could posses; that one could observe the reaction of another, adjust one's behavior, frame one's response in such a way as to influence the other person to get a better result. He felt exposed, delightfully.

Rue took some time to talk about what was happening in his family, the abuse of his sister, the financial stress on his parents and their marriage, and his "creative way of showing just how fucking tired he was of it all," by staging his own murder with the glove and knife.

Rue got him; she really saw him. Jacob hadn't realized it, but he had staged a violent attack. He wondered if she knew it was about more than Melody and his parents. That he was also killing off bits of himself wedged in the past so that new parts could grow in, like a reptile regenerating a new limb.

"Jacob, are you aware of what it means to be mesmerized?"

"Like, to be in a trance?"

"Yes, that's exactly right. Someone, Jacob, has put you under a spell." Rue sat still like a placid, blue lake.

"Who?" Jacob asked. "A spell like a witch makes?"

Rue crossed her legs and placed her folded hands on her knee. "Someone has bewitched you into believing you have to protect them, and it's costing you a lot."

"You know? How did you know?"

"The next time we meet, we'll find out more about

this spell and this witch. Would you like that?"

"Can I hug you?"

Rue embraced him. He began to pat her back.

"Jacob, there's no need to pat. Just receive. Let me do the patting."

Jacob relaxed into her body. She was warm, like fresh-baked bread.

A book on her shelf caught his eye: *The Architecture of Wizardry*.

"Are those magic books?"

"People-magic, not magic tricks," said Rue.

"What's people-magic?"

"Those books won't teach you how to pull rabbits out of hats, Jacob. They're about the structure of therapeutic communication; how change happens."

"Can I borrow one?"

"I don't usually loan my books out, and they might be a little advanced for you."

"I read the Power of Positive Thinking by Norman Vincent Peale when I was eight-years-old. I'd like to give it a shot."

Rue howled. She looked at Jacob and perceived a seriousness, a yearning for truth, a mind that was open and eager; she saw a disciple.

"I'll tell you what, Jacob, take it, read what you can. Come back next week, and we'll discuss it." ❧

CHAPTER XI

People Magic

Jacob read the cover of "The Architecture of Wizardry: a book about words and how they can help people." He wanted to help people. As he turned the page, he thought of Jonathan Livingston Seagull, flapping; swooping; learning. He thought about the way the bird ascended; hovered; tilted, scraping its wing across the sky; how he became fearless; now teaching other birds to help themselves. Jacob could see the seagull clearly; that satisfied him. The bird wore a gray-feathered flight jacket over his white plumes; the black crest on his head was like a helmet. His red-orange beak pierced the wind.

Jacob kept reading. His hand lingered above the page like a hawk soaring on a thermal, suspended, waiting for the signal to dive and turn. There was a warning. The book promised tools to make the reader a better therapist, but cautioned that humans don't perceive the world directly; they are only able to interact using their senses, which create impressions, or models of the world.

People are like programmed characters moving through a video game, thought Jacob. He imagined himself in Rue's chair, helping people change their programming.

Then he was reading quickly again, eager to get to the techniques, but the rest of the warning slowed him down. One must mitigate the pitfalls of being an entity that doesn't operate in the real world but through imperfect models. How freeing! How frightful! Jacob lowered the book. His wide forehead relaxed. His small mouth opened into a circle. His brown eyes gazed at the book's cover: a white-bearded wizard in a black robe, frozen in a whirl among green and purple ether, pointing a wand.

If everybody on the planet is working off these mental models, then nobody really knows what they're doing. Models can be updated, changed, improved, thrown out, thought Jacob. Religions are models, families are models, bodies are models, time is a model.

All ideas of reality and the world changed for Jacob in that opening warning, as if the words had been written in bold, red letters.

"Your model of the world is not the world itself," said Rue. Jacob remembered to keep his feet from scraping the camelhair rug. Under his breath, he repeated her sentence like a mantra.

"Yeah, I'm not sure I fully understand it," said Jacob.

"Can you think of some examples from your own experience?" Rue snuffed out her Benson & Hedges in the green swirly ashtray and leaned forward in her big chair.

"What about when I couldn't find a toy, and it was right in front of me all along?"

"That's a wonderful example. In *The Architecture of Wizardry*, Axler and Miller would call that a deletion. You made a negative hallucination of the object you wanted to see. And that's a great illustration of how your model of the world, at that moment, was impoverished."

"Impoverished?"

"Missing pieces," said Rue.

"What do we do about it?"

Rue laughed until she coughed. In Jacob's question, she recognized the innocence and openness of a student ready to be taught. Then, settling, preening slightly, Rue crossed a leg over a knee. She looked like Saraswati on her white goose, radiating, with lute in hand (it was really a slender, white cigarette) appearing to float in front of Jacob. He sat with his palms upon his lap as if he were showing himself completely, without defensiveness and worry. Rue perceived Jacob was loosening his stubborn grip on his model of reality.

Resident in him was something greater than personal potential, she thought, as his shoulders dropped and his face relaxed as if she had seen fall all around him lotus petals of pink, purple, and white. Jacob had an uncanny power of perception. He was wise. He was unrelenting. He was tormented. If she didn't guide him, he would devour the patterns on his own and become a monster—like the Zburător—young, charming, and all possessing.

"The task for us is to learn how to learn how to learn."

Jacob's brown eyes exploded with a vision. "Yes, I get

that! So we can know things we don't know, and what we don't know, we can go find out so that we know them." He was up and pacing.

Rue clapped her hands and jumped up out of her chair. "Dear God, you're just a child. But you might be able to grasp it. We're talking about Bateson, here, Jacob. This is called Learning Three—learning how to learn how to learn."

"Learning Three," Jacob repeated. "This is how people can get better, isn't it?"

"Indeed it is," said Rue. "Problems can be fixed by learning new things and unlearning old things."

They poured over more questions Jacob had from the first chapter. Rue suggested he continue reading the book, paying particular attention to the chapters on how language shapes one's perception of reality.

"If language shapes perception, can it unshape it?" asked Jacob.

"An astute listener can ask questions to challenge perceptions. If powerful enough, those questions indeed change perceptions," said Rue.

"If you ask me the right questions, can you break the spell my mom has on me?"

"Ask and you shall receive, love."

Rue looked at Jacob, but didn't see a client. She recognized maternal feelings she hadn't experienced since her daughter Lucy had died.

"You aren't responsible for your mother, Jacob. It's the other way around."

Jacob caught his foot about to swipe across the camelhair rug. "I wish you were my mom. What is this stuff called that you do, Rue? It feels like magic."

"It did to me too, love." She smiled as she sat back in her chair. Her blue eyes flashed to the ceiling and back to Jacob's face as she reached for another cigarette. "I'll tell you, I was coming apart after Preston told me he was divorcing me. We'd just lost our daughter, Lucy to cancer. My practice at The Center was suffering. Little did I know I was being pushed out of there. Hedges Capers was telling me to get out on my own, but I had the belief I always needed a man to make it in this world. Then I heard about this week-long seminar in Miami about a therapy called Quantum Change by Raymond Axler and James Miller. I didn't know who they were or what Quantum Change was, but Capers said to go, so I did."

Rue reminded Jacob of Yoda. When she spoke, he didn't feel little, and she didn't seem old. She talked to him like he was a person. He didn't understand everything she said, but somehow, one day, he knew he would.

"At one point in the seminar, Axler called me up to the stage," she continued. "He mispronounced my name. I corrected him, and he said, 'I'm Raymond Axler, and I'll call you whatever the hell I want.' I said, 'Yes, sir,' and floated up the aisle. Later at the bar, he asked me if I'd be his spokesperson for media events. I said, 'But Raymond, the media aren't even here.' He said, 'They will be. Do you want the job or not?' I've been in the inner circle ever since."

"I want to go to a seminar one day," said Jacob.

"I'm sure you will, love."

Jacob wanted desperately to read every book there was about Quantum Change; to watch Rue work with other clients; to become a master at changing people. He had observed Rue maneuver around his mother's antics. But she was doing more. She used her body and her voice, and he needed to find out what else was happening.

"In our family sessions, I've been noticing you copycat the person you're talking to. Like, if their legs are crossed, you cross yours," Jacob told Rue, who held her cigarette in the air, suspended, as if waiting for the word "Action" to come from an off-stage director. "Or if they fold their hands, you fold yours. So I've been practicing that, trying to notice how people act. It's weird because it makes them talk to me more, and I feel more comfortable."

"It's a technique called Mirroring. It helps build rapport at the unconscious level. You figured this out by watching me in family session?"

"Yeah, and there's something else, too. You do it a lot when you're trying to get my mom to change her mind, like when you want to influence her. So today, I got in trouble again for not dressing out. I started mirroring my coach right away. His arms were crossed; he looked really upset. After a bit, I uncrossed my arms, and he uncrossed his too. Then I said he should realize that P.E. is hard for me, and he could just let it go. And he did!"

"Jesus, God! You're combining skills. You took Mirroring to a deeper level. There's no reason we can't get you into a certification training. How would you like that, love?"

"I'd like it very much. I know they're expensive, but maybe I can raise some funds. I can use Christmas and birthday money and see if Uncle Tommy would help cover the rest."

"I'll ask Raymond if there are any scholarship slots open for the next Tampa workshop. As far as I know, you'd be the youngest practitioner to be certified in Quantum Change."

Jacob heard every word his father said, though muffled as if Edwin had been speaking them from behind a wall. For they were too painful for Jacob to let them be in the same room with him, much less enter his brain all at once.

Perhaps it was the fear God was punishing him for taking his focus away from the debt he owed Christ, and that his disconnection from the church might soon bring destruction to him and his family.

Or maybe it was the weight of loneliness he had to bear in the presence of his mother when his father was gone; she looked to Jacob for comfort and for safety. "Brush my hair," she'd whine. "Rub my feet." "Get Mommy a glass of tea." "Massage my neck." She expected constant servitude, leaving him feeling greasy and dirty because he was being made to play an unnatural part.

"Jacob, did you hear your father?" demanded Rose.

He had. The furniture business had been sold. The house was on the market, but there were no offers. Their plan to move was going slower than they'd hoped. Now they had to dip into their nest egg. Therefore, Edwin had accepted a job selling golf clubs and bags. But there was no market in central Florida, so he would have to be on the road for weeks at a time in south Florida.

"I'll come home one or two weekends a month," Edwin promised Jacob.

Jacob couldn't fall asleep while Edwin was away. He tried counting sheep as his mother suggested, but once he drifted off his creative mind turned the pastoral scene of grazing lambs into a gore-fest where the drove was hunted by wolves, which turned into werewolves, which spiraled into bloody images of his father dead on the road. Sometimes he could convince Melody to sleep in his bed, but if Rose caught them the next morning she tore into a frenzy on account of the molestation, worrying about the damage the effect a brother and sister sleeping with each other might have on a victim ("victim" was the new word in the household now; a role Rose was keen to cast herself in). On occasion, Jacob would crawl into his mother's bed, which she allowed. She stayed up late watching Carson, then The Late Show. She usually fell asleep before he did.

Rose told Edwin about Jacob's nightmares. After church one Sunday, they sat him down.

"We want you to know, son everything will be okay," promised Rose. "Your father and I prayed about him being gone so much and the nightmares you've been having. While we were praying, a miracle happened."

"We were down on our knees, and a bright light filled the room," said Edwin.

"Filled the room, how?" asked Jacob.

"This white light suddenly entered the room through our window; it was an angel. God was telling us the house will sell soon, and everything will be fine. We'll all be together again, and I won't be away from you. You don't need to worry." Edwin held Rose's hand and patted Jacob's head.

"How, specifically, do you know it was an angel? Maybe it was the glare of headlights."

"Jacob, don't pull that Quantum shit on us. There were no cars on that back road. You need to trust us."

"Okay, dad. It was a white light, an angel. That's really amazing."

"Don't you believe in God anymore?" asked Rose. Her voice trembled. She wrung her hands.

"Of course I do. It's just—I really want the house to sell, and I'm excited the angel told you it will happen soon."

Did an angel visit his parents? He couldn't imagine one did. They wanted to see an angel. Or maybe they were making up the whole thing, pretending to have had a religious experience to try to encourage him. If the house did sell soon, it proved nothing.

Months later, Jacob's family drove to Tampa to a Catholic bookstore. Faith, Elaine's sister, mentioned to Edwin that if one were to bury a statue of St. Joseph upside down, facing the house, and threaten the holy father of Jesus, saying, "I will keep you face down in the dirt until you sell my house for me," the house would get an offer quickly.

During Joseph's burial, Jacob didn't press his parents to find out if this ritual was part of the angel's plan. ❧

CHAPTER XII

A Silver Lining

"I know Daddy did something to me too," Rose told Rue, wadding her tissue into a ball. "I've had a memory, but it was only of a kiss. I don't think it was anything else. I can't imagine he meant to hurt Melody. Maybe he only touched her by accident."

"A touch can be hurtful, Rose. And the mind can bury memories that are painful. I'd like to use hypnosis to help you remember more."

"I don't want to do that," her voice raised a pitch. "I'm afraid." She squeezed her legs together.

"I see that, love. And I hear there's an awful lot that needs protecting. And Melody needs your protection. She needs to know you support her."

"We have been supporting her. We're paying you by the hour, aren't we? I don't need to confront Daddy and make Mama mad, get the whole family stirred up over this. He's gonna be gone before we know it." Rose shredded the tissue in her lap.

So there in Rue's condo, in the dim, yellow lamplight, as a helix of blue smoke from the Benson & Hedges wound round itself pushing up toward the rafters, and a halfhearted rain dallied with the palm trees along the Hillsborough River, Rose decided to make-believe life was not so bad. She had learned to survive the Ramburg household; she could protect her daughter. She could admit (to herself) she was too late to prevent the tragedies that happened, but she vowed (to herself) to stay vigilant from now on.

Rue watched this dark conciliation creep across Rose's face like life passing from a drowning woman's last gasp for air—out goes the color, the water stills, all is quiet; the face goes placid and ceraceous, the eyes stare.

"Will you go to the family reunion next month?"

"We damn sure will," said Rose. "With our pride."

Rue's eyebrow curled. "Back to the same place where Melody begged you to save her?"

"I will be with her this time. Besides, they've bought a new cabin on a mountain; they made an addition for us to sleep in. It'll give her some distance."

"It sounds like you're justifying a dangerous decision, Rose."

"Fuck you. This session is over."

As soon as Rose stormed out, Rue phoned Edwin. For when a client walked out of a session in a huff, it meant the therapeutic contract was over. But because of her love for Jacob and Melody, she had allowed herself to be taken hostage.

"I'll stay in this for their sake," she told him. "Don't

take this child to North Carolina. That man is a monster. You have to make a choice between your daughter and your wife, and in this case, Edwin, you must choose your daughter. If you don't, you'll lose her to something far worse than Klaus Ramburg."

"Mom, why do they call it a silver lining?" asked Jacob.

Rose's eye caught the folded pair of jeans on the dresser. She had put them there the night before to remember to pack them.

"There's an old saying, 'Every cloud has a silver lining.' It means no matter how bad things get, there's always hope." Her mood elevated, became aerial, dizzyingly, at the thought of arriving at the mountains. "Maw Maw and Grandaddy wanted to have more room for the whole family when we visit, so they bought a big travel trailer and attached it to a cabin. They call it The Silver Lining because family is their hope."

"And the thing is silver?" Jacob imagined an old-fashioned bomber, like the Enola Gay, stripped of its wings and tail section, fastened to the side of a mountain cabin.

"All silver," said Rose.

The unknown always hung over Jacob. And as he was sorting out his questions, and as he had been indoctrinated that his mother was the only one on whom he could rely, and as his thoughts began to spiral, Jacob grasped for all the options, so now, he could create a simulacrum of the future, adding details here, imagination there, like window dressing and mannequins in a department store window. "And big enough for Uncle Donald's whole family, too?"

"No, they want to stay in a roadside motel. They'll fit for meals though."

"But what if our house sells while we're gone this summer?"

"The realtor will take care of it."

What if the realtor doesn't call? What if we have a car accident on our vacation? What if—He clicked his teeth and nodded his head through the bad thoughts until he could visualize everything going just right.

Click teeth, nod, lock the good thought in place.

Jacob read the clean, white sign just down the road from a little church on the creek. *Hiawatha Cabin Park* popped out in brightly painted blue letters. Edwin parked the van and rolled down his window. He was immediately greeted by Gene Cowper, the park owner.

"Hello there. Can I help you?"

"Yes, sir. We're Klaus and Audrey Ramburg's family."

"Well, of course you are. We've all been expecting you."

As the men spoke, the Smokey Mountains pressed all around with a vast force. The branches of the tall Pignut hickory trees fanned up and down. Puffy clouds seemed stuffed behind the leaves, like quilt batting. The smell of Cottonwood trees would forever link Jacob to this place and time.

He heard footsteps slapping up the path behind the van. It was a tall boy in blue corduroy Ocean Pacific shorts and a cotton-white shirt. He put his arm around his grandfather. He wasn't out of breath from the running. Jolting out a hip and resting a hand on it, he grinned widely as he tried to peer in the van.

What was he looking for? Jacob wondered. The boy waved wildly. His long, thin fingers blended together in a flash. Jacob liked his white palms and bony elbows. The tan lines on his arms and neck revealed his paler complexion.

"This is my grandson," said Mr. Cowper.

"Hi, I'm Blake. Blake Wolf." He leaned on Edwin's window craning his head all the way into the van. Jacob smiled.

"That's my son Jacob," Edwin shook his hand. "It's nice to meet you, Blake. Jacob, say hello. Introduce yourself."

Jacob only waved.

"It's okay if he's shy. I'm not. Anyway, I'm glad you're here. I've been hopin' someone would show up my age to hang out with. Wanna come down after while?"

"Now Blake, he just got here, and his grandparents are gonna want to see him—"

"Yeah, I'll be down in a bit," said Jacob.

"Cool. I'll show ya the creek. We can go fishin'."

"I want to come too," said Melody, suddenly as perky as a puppy.

But Jacob wanted Blake all to himself. He hoped Blake would see it that way too.

"Sure, you can come sweetie."

Jacob tried to be disappointed, but the boy who was tender with his sister might have a good heart; he might be a good boy who could be a real friend.

The Murtaugh's van wound around the forested drive

up the mountain. Mr. Cowper had strategically placed white painted signs every few hundred yards. Bold red and blue letters advertised God's love (or wrath) for those traveling through his park: *For God so loved the world that He gave His only Son. John 3:16; Repent now for the Kingdom of God is at hand; Turn to Jesus before it's too late!* And, *God hates the sin, not the sinner.*

On the pinnacle of the mountain, Jacob saw a wedge of sunlight leaning against the sterling-plated appendage next to the Ramburg's cabin. *So that's The Silver Lining.* He found the scene smaller than what his mind had built (it was more of a lodge), but he was accustomed to life not measuring up.

Rose embraced Audrey, then kissed Klaus; Jacob's curiosity about how his mother would act after Melody's revelation was now quelled. The Ramburgs had not been informed of the accusations. Whenever they called, Rose or Edwin made excuses not to talk, and the Murtaughs were always a no-show at family birthdays and luncheons. Rue had been pushing for an intervention with Klaus, but Rose kept stalling.

If Audrey suspected something was off, she didn't show it. And here was Rose, able to escape into a new fantasy of her parents, pretending in her mind a new beginning, insisting untreated wounds had magically healed by apologies that never came.

Melody pretended, too (taking her cue from Rose). She kissed Audrey and Klaus, said how happy she was to be here. If she remembered it was Audrey who had cleaned her up after Klaus was done with her, that was far in the back of her mind. School was going well. Yes, she got the card they sent and thank you. No, she hadn't outgrown the blouse. Yes, she liked the color.

"We'll, ya'll must be exhausted. Come inside and see the new place," Audrey said. She needed to show every detail; how Klaus had built this cabinet, refinished that table and countertop; she had made the curtains, "Notice the strawberry pattern. Don't you like them?" Yes, everyone thought the strawberries were a nice touch. There was a shop down the road that reupholstered the diner, set in red leather to match the strawberry pattern. They had put down new carpet and found a good deal on a pullout couch.

"Jacob and Melody, wait 'til you see yall's room. And you have your own bathroom."

Everything was a distraction, senseless talk. Jacob wanted to run. *What was Blake doing?* He wanted to work the conversation around to the part where he asked to go play with Blake, but didn't want to hurt Audrey's feelings. "Mr. Cowper's grandson is nice."

"He's very nice. He's a good Christian boy," said Audrey. "He helped Gene put up all those signs a few weeks back."

"He wants to show me the creek, said he'd take me fishing."

"Well, not right now, honey, you just got here, and Maw Maw wants to see you," she said and laughed to ease his letdown.

"Let him go," said Klaus.

Audrey opened her mouth to protest, but Klaus' glare cut her off.

"Well, be back for dinner. You can bring him with you."

"Thanks, Maw Maw!"

"Take your sister," said Rose.

Melody and Jacob ran out the door and headed down the path toward Mr. and Mrs. Cowper's house.

"You okay?" asked Jacob. "Seeing him again after so long?"

"Yeah, but I want the bottom bunk; I don't want to crawl up on the top one," said Melody.

"Okay, fine. But if Blake wants to hang out, just me and him sometime, you have to let us. You gotta find your own things to do."

"No, I don't. If Mommy says, you have to take me."

Jacob read a small white sign stuck in the ground: *No dogs allowed.* Jacob pointed to it. "See that? No dogs, Melody."

"That's mean. I'm gonna tell Mommy you're being inappropriate (she had learned that word from Rue). And there's no one here for me to play with."

"You can play with Lena or Carol Alice when they get here."

"But I don't like them."

"Neither do I, but that's not my problem."

"They're no fun. Please let me hangout with you, Bubba."

"Sometimes you can. Just not all the time. Understand? There he is. Now be quiet," said Jacob.

Blake visited Hiawatha Park every summer to help his grandparents but lived with his mother on a mountain in nearby Cullowhee. He walked fast and spoke through a permanent smile.

"You ready for some mountain fun?"

His invitation sounded dangerous and exciting.

"Where are we going?" asked Jacob.

"I'm not telling. You're gonna have to trust me."

They crossed the lazy road in front of the park; it hosted a car only once in a while. At the creek, Blake showed off his skills skipping rocks and crossing felled trees barefoot. Jacob was afraid to try. He didn't want to fall in the water.

"Don't tell me you're a chicken, Jacob. Or should I call you Jake?" Melody scampered out on the log and started to lose her balance. Blake reached out his hand to support her.

"I don't like risky stuff. And I hate when people call me Jake. My Nana calls me Jay."

"What do ya'll do in the big city, Jay?" Jacob liked how he mocked. He had an edge, but it was mixed with a large dose of friendliness.

"You've never been to Florida? There's Disney and Sea World. We've been there lots."

"Nah, we're poor," Blake said without shame.

"So what do you do up here? Skip rocks and crawl on trees?" Jacob matched his jesting style, a rapport-building technique he learned from Rue.

Blake laughed. "Not feelin' so shy now, huh?"

That was what he wanted—for Blake to goad him until he wasn't shy; the tightness in his chest and throat would release. Now he would say things he couldn't say before.

Jacob balanced both feet on the log. He knew what Blake was thinking, *Just get on the log and I'll help you.* He wanted to feel the palm of Blake's hand, to feel if it was as soft as it looked. Jacob inched further along the log, wavering.

Blake leapt onto the tree and extended his hand.

151

"You're not going to make it across by yourself."

Jacob felt Blake's body shading him like a cloud passing across the sun.

"No, I can't," said Jacob, staring past the log at the ground below. Blake was still looking at him, but his expression changed. He wanted Blake to say something to him—the thing no boy could dare say to another boy.

Jacob kept his eyes on the log; Blake understood.

"Hold my hand," he said.

The crossed together, smiling.

"Your family sure seems nice." Blake spat on a fern giving the plant a good shake.

"Don't let 'em fool ya," said Jacob. "What are your mom and dad like?"

"My mom's the best thing in my life. My dad's a deadbeat. My step-dad is okay. He's good to my mom, so I like him. What grade you goin' into?"

"Seventh. I may have to start a new school, though, if our house sells and we move."

The house will sell. Everything is okay.

"Seventh is easy. I'm goin' into eighth. That's where things really start up." From anyone else this would sound like a competition, but Jacob forgot his insecurities, feeling a little drunk on Blake's intensity.

"I'm going into second grade," announced Melody. "It's going to be fun, but I'll be scared if we start new schools, and I'll be scared because I won't be at the same school as my bubba."

"Bubba? She calls you Bubba?" Blake slapped his leg. "We don't even call people that up here."

Jacob noticed the sun setting. "Dinner! Maw Maw

wants us home. You want to eat with us tonight? My grandmother is a good cook; she said you could come."

"Let's stop by my granny's so she'll know not to fix me somethin.'"

Klaus grilled hamburgers and hot dogs in the front yard. Audrey arranged placemats on the picnic table and shouted directions to Rose in the kitchen. Edwin picked the weeds in the flowerbed. When Melody and the boys walked up the driveway, Audrey waved and welcomed Blake to the table.

At dinner, Jacob watched Blake. He hunkered over his burger and took fast bites as if someone was going to steal it. Jacob liked to watch him eat, talk, climb; Blake could do anything, or nothing, and Jacob would want to watch.

Blake accompanied the Murtaughs wherever they went: horseback excursions, fishing trips, picnics along the Blue Ridge Parkway, swimming trips to Sliding Rock in Pisgah National Forest; Blake experienced parts of his own state he had never seen before. But what was best was the two boys together. They sat in the back of the Chevy Astro on the bench seat, side by side, bare knees touching, talking about everything.

Rose watched them and worried. She wondered if it was normal for boys to be so close. No point in asking Edwin, she thought to herself. For his view of Jacob is obstructed, he sees through frosted glass; everything has soft edges. Discussing her suspicions would be impossible the way he pretends not to notice the problems with Jacob.

I need someone who sees the way I do.

Her speculations boiled over when Blake suggested Jacob should spend the night at the Cowper's.

"You're getting too old for sleepovers," Rose said.

"You didn't sleep over at your friends when you were my age?" Jacob sat on the sofa and tried to sound curious.

"Yes, but I'm a girl."

"Dad, did you have sleep—"

"Don't involve your father in this," said Rose, leaning over to pinch Jacob's cheek.

"Let go. That hurts."

"Lower your voice, Jacob."

"Rose, leave that boy be. Let him spend the night if he wants," yelled Audrey from the sink.

"Where will you sleep?" Rose asked.

"With Blake," said Jacob.

"You're too old to share a bed. One of you should sleep on the floor."

"I'll leave that up to Mrs. Cowper."

Jacob was out the door and down the hill before Rose had a chance to sling another objection.

But there was hardly any sleeping. The two watched MTV until they fell asleep near daylight. Blake was up not long after to do his chores. Jacob felt around for him in the bed, missed him sorely when he noticed he was gone, got up, and found Mrs. Cowper had made breakfast for him.

The next night, Blake had a plan.

"Have you ever played Dungeons and Dragons?"

"Not really. Never got into it," said Jacob.

"Will you try it with me?"

"Only with you."

They sat at a large table. The thick, slick wood was streaked with hues of black and red-orange. It was a hell-table, Jacob thought.

"There's a bunch of characters in D & D; it can get complicated," said Blake.

"You really think you can teach me to play?" Jacob picked through figurines and odd-shaped black and red dice. "I don't think I've taken enough math to understand this game."

"Don't worry. It's the story that matters. Focus on the story and your character. Those are your guides. And I'll be the DM, the Dungeon Master. I won't go hard on you the first time." Blake didn't wink, but smiled in a way that would make you swear he had.

"So, what kind of character do you want to be?"

Jacob was crippled. Idiocy set in, like rigor. He searched for ideas like one stumbles in a dark room feeling for the door. "I dunno. Can't you pick for me?"

"Yeah. I've got a character from another campaign that's perfect. You're gonna be a fifth-level Wizard named Orthanach. I'm starting you off high so it won't be boring."

"Should I thank you?"

"Wizards are cool; it fits you. You've got some potions, a staff, and a magic wand, of course."

"What do you play as?"

"I'm always DM."

I'M always *DM.* Jacob repeated the words to himself.

I'm ALWAYS DM.

I'm always DM. How had he said it? Emphasis on the DM. Who says only he gets to be the DM? It sounds like

S & M. An unexpected image of Blake whipped through Jacob's mind.

"Are you gonna daydream or are we playing?" asked Blake.

"I'm ready—Master."

"Good slave. Let's begin." Blake clasped his hands and rested them on the table. He leaned toward Jacob. One bushy black brow raised into a curl. Shadowy dunes, as if seen from orbit, took shape on his forehead. "It's 15th century Ireland. Orthanach is a young Wizard, but he's already earned the trust of the Mayor. He's got a weakness for the Meade, so he's in a tavern called Luain's. Suddenly, the roar of laughter and music comes to a halt when someone runs into the tavern and screams, 'The Mayor's daughter's been kidnapped by Bandits.' Like nothing happened, the music starts up again and people are laughing. What do you do?"

Blake's eyes reflected the candleshine like polished mahogany.

"What are my options?" asked Jacob. "Order another drink and not worry about it, I say."

"That would be a short game," said Blake. "Orthanach cares about the Mayor's family. He would want to help."

"How 'bout I follow the guy out to the alley and ask him who captured the mayor's daughter."

"Perfect. 'Truth be told,' says the guy, 'The Mayor let 'em walk right out with her.' Me don't know anythin' else, lad.' What do you want to do now?"

"I could follow him; see where he goes."

"Orthanach is a powerful Wizard. He's not going to waste time like that."

"I could shoot him with my wand," said Jacob.

"Don't waste a spell on this guy. It probably won't help. Why not go talk to the Mayor."

"Okay, I want to go to the Mayor's house," said Jacob.

"It's the fifteenth century. He lives in a castle."

Blake flipped through a book and tapped on the page dealing with spells. "You're gonna need some of these. Read up quick because you've just come across a fierce guard in front of the castle door. What do you do?"

"I want to hit him with a Magic Missile."

Blake rolled the dice. "Thirteen points of damage on the guard. Now the guard swings a truncheon and hits you. He does sixteen points of non-lethal damage, leaving you at four points. I suggest you surrender, Orthanach."

"Why?"

"Because there's another guard who's going to swing on you now."

"Okay, I surrender!"

"But you get captured and put in prison. What do you wish to do?"

"What kind of prison am I in?"

"You're in luck. It's not a prison of four stone walls. The prison is an iron cage."

"I wanna use the Knock spell and get out," said Jacob.

"Fine. Just remember, once you've used a spell, you'll forget it. Are you sure?" Blake asked.

Jacob was intimidated; feeling he was in Blake's hands; lost in a world in which he had no control. Jacob was aroused. No one else was there to notice him poised, bound, absorbed. No one else was there to notice the need that had descended upon him earnestly. No one else was there to guess his only wish was to offer himself like waves throwing themselves upon the rocks.

"Knock," said Jacob.

Blake was pleased. "The door is open. But a guard comes toward you."

"Shit, can't you give a Wizard a break?" Jacob looked over the spells. "Maybe I can get intel from him. I want to use the suggestion spell."

"All right, go for it."

"You should tell me where the Mayor's daughter is so you won't get punished later." "The guard tells you, 'The daughter of the mayor was sacrificed so the pillaging would cease.'"

"What pillaging?" asked Jacob.

"It seems the Chieftain bandit has been attacking your village's trading caravans. The Mayor cut a deal: peace for pussy. You've got to find out where she is. What do you do?"

"I suggest to the guard, 'If you run away and come back later you'd probably save your life.'"

"You're catching on. But you can't use the same spell again, remember? And to make matters worse, while you've been dallying, the Chieftain has brought in an evil cleric who is about to force the daughter to marry him."

"So I'll find the Mayor and offer to trade my invisibility potion for the location of his daughter."

"Okay, that works. The Mayor accepts your trade offer and reveals the location of the Chieftain's compound."

Mrs. Cowper yelled for Blake. It was time for dinner.

They promised to play again later that night, but with Blake, every moment was like turning a corner onto an unforeseen landscape, always abrupt, always an anagram of implications.

When they said goodbye for the summer, Rose watched critically.

As they hugged Blake said, "If you write me, I'll write you."

"Are you using a suggestion spell on me?" asked Jacob.

"Do I have to?" asked Blake, and then handed Jacob something and whispered in his ear.

Edwin felt bad for his son. He recalled parting with friends and cousins he only saw when he visited Brooklyn. He thought about a couple of the boys in Nam. Rose reached over and honked the horn.

"Can't you be a little sensitive?" said Edwin. "Give him some space."

"Why doesn't he act that way around girls?" Rose asked out loud.

"So critical," Edwin sighed. "You have to be so critical. Just like your mother."

Rose wanted to scream. She caught Melody watching her. She clenched her teeth and decided to bring it up with Edwin later in the hotel room. ❧

CHAPTER XIII

Cabin Fever

Jacob and Blake kept in touch during the year by phone and letters. Rose resisted opening and reading them, except for one:

> *I miss you and your argumentative sister, your finger-biting father, and your mother who has the funkiest son I know of. Hope to see you soon.*
>
> *Love,*
>
> *Your best hillbilly friend (and the greatest DM in the world),*
> Blake

Rose eavesdropped on one of the boys' phone calls. Jacob had responded, "I love you too," to which Rose pursed her lips and raised an eyebrow. She referenced the letter and phone call with the tone of a lawyer entering evidence in court.

"Jacob, it's not normal for boys to tell each other they love each other."

Sitting between his mother and father on the couch, Jacob stiffened like one does before getting a shot.

"It is too, Rose. You don't know what you're talking about," said Edwin,

"I've had lots of guy friends, and we said, 'I love you.'"

Rose rolled her eyes. There was no revelation in that.

Jacob was afraid she was right; maybe it was odd. But he couldn't unlock the mystery of what Blake meant by "love." It wasn't worth troubling himself about when Blake wrote it; anyone and everyone said that in a letter. But Jacob was caught off guard when he heard Blake say it on the phone. And he paused as if he was waiting to hear it back.

Unsatisfied with Jacob's explanation that he and Blake were best friends, Rose drug him into Rue's office to air her complaint.

"Jacob made a friend in North Carolina, and there's something off about it. He's not telling me something, Rue."

"Well, I wouldn't either, Rose if you forced me in here like a slave. Jesus-God have some respect for the boy!"

"They tell each other, 'I love you,' in letters and on the phone like they're gay or something."

Jacob hid his face in his hands.

"Get out of my office, Rose. Come back in an hour to pick up your son."

"But I need to—"

Rue pointed at Rose. "If you say another word child,

you'll leave him here overnight with me. Get out now."

"Jacob, would you please tell me about your friend. You certainly care about him. And if he's someone you care about, he must be a special person."

Jacob described how much he missed Blake, their adventures, his companionship, how he changed his mind like a fickle cat, how compassionate he was to Melody.

"Everyone other friend seems inferior; we don't keep secrets from each other."

"I'm so glad, Jacob, you've finally met a friend like Blake. And love takes many forms. Your mother is paranoid about love. Don't let her fear become yours."

"What do you think Blake means when he tells me he loves me?"

"I can't know what Blake or anyone thinks, love. I failed mind-reading in school. If you want to know, you have to ask him."

"What do I do about missing him so much?"

"Distance is hard. Recreate your time together by taking part in something you did with him in North Carolina here in Florida."

The next summer when the Murtaughs rolled into Hiawatha Cabin Park, Blake didn't greet them.

"Let me out, I want to find him," said Jacob.

"Not until you see your grandparents," said Rose.

"I know you're rearin' to see Blake, but he's not here yet, Jacob. His mama's been real sick, and he's at home takin' care of her," said Audrey.

He had made sure he didn't look at his mother, so she wouldn't get sick too. *Click teeth and nod at the wall. Everyone is okay.*

Jacob telephoned Blake. "I'm sorry to hear about your mom. I wish you were here. It's weird without you."

"Same here. What are you going to do on all those horseback trips and whitewater rafting tours without me?"

He would be miserable, that's what.

"So you're not coming at all?" Jacob's voice must've wavered.

"We'll see. Don't worry, Jay, if not this year, there's always next year." Blake's optimism wasn't genuine.

Jacob woke one Sunday morning to Klaus shaking his foot.

"Wake up, boy. You're coming to church with me today."

"I am? It's so early, Grandaddy."

"I said get up, let's go."

Jacob got dressed.

"You need a tie. Wear this one." Klaus handed him a brown tie with a blue diamond pattern. "Board!"

Yelling "Board" was Klaus' usual manner of indicating it was time to go. Whoever was going with him had better drop what they were doing and get out the door.

Klaus and Jacob walked to the Baptist church by the creek in silence. From the church's open windows, Jacob could hear people singing, "How Great Thou Art," which he thought was a fitting soundtrack for the mountains that surrounded the valley. When they walked in, he saw Mr. Cowper, and that boy with the brown hair, taller now, in a silver-blue suit sitting next to his grandfather. The door slammed behind Jacob. Blake turned around, smiled and waved, then got up and jogged down the aisle. The boys hugged, faces pressed cheek to cheek.

After the service, Klaus and Mr. Cowper went to Bible study. Blake and Jacob went to Sunday school. But the Good news did not come because of religion that day.

"I'm here the rest of the time you are. And guess what, Jay, Granny's given us our own cabin. Just you and me."

"That means we can come and go as we please and not have to worry about waking anybody up," said Jacob.

"Yeah, and play D & D all night. And we don't have to share a bed either," Blake said. Jacob was disappointed. He liked waking up in the middle of the night with Blake's knee between his thighs, or his hand laying across his chest. He wondered if Blake pointed this out to test his reaction.

"It wasn't that big of a deal, at least I didn't think so," said Jacob.

"Nah, it wasn't. We don't have to use the other bed. We could save her the trouble of making up both beds."

Jacob was learning the nuances of communication from Rue, but he missed Blake's hint. He had not yet grasped the subtlety of indirect talk.

Often Blake brought up sexual topics and Jacob eagerly engaged, but he didn't know how to show he was interested in going to the next level, the level beyond talk.

In their private cabin, Blake opened a cabinet in the dining room.

"Come over here," he said. He lit a candle on the table. He lit another on top of the television. Another on the

165

coffee table, and kept this up until there were eight lit in all. A gust of wind billowed the curtains and threatened the flames. They withstood, returning erect, hot, and yellow. There was no hell-table, but Jacob knew what Blake was preparing.

"Do you remember where we left off, Orthanach?" asked Blake.

"I suggest you remind me," said Jacob.

Blake took out the character sheet and a list of spells. "You had just traded the Mayor a potion to find his daughter. She's being held at the Chieftain's hideout and is about to be forced to marry him. Your move."

"I, Orthanach have arrived at the hideout. I intend—"

"You are greeted by a bulwark of guards, six of them, and they're coming at you fast."

"I cast a Wall of Fire spell and divide them into three," said Jacob.

"The three guards behind the wall are dead," said Blake. "The other three are advancing."

"You could hand me your sword if I promise to give it back later."

"Is that a suggestion?" asked Blake.

"Yeah, I have that spell, right?"

"It's been a year. You totally do. But it's a little Freudian, don't you think?"

"How so?"

"You want some guy to put his sword in your hand?"

"Very funny, DM. Does he do it or not?"

"The guard hands you his weapon," said Blake.

"I throw it and fight all three with my staff."

"You took on some damage, but they're dead. Nice

work. So how do you handle your sword, Jay?"

"Like every other guy, I guess. There's more than one way? How else do you do it?" Jacob asked.

"I can't tell you because you'll go try it and hurt yourself. You have to really know the technique."

"I won't try it, I promise." Out it came, too soon. He promised just to keep Blake talking about how he masturbated.

"Sorry I can't tell you. It takes the right touch."

"Okay, fine, you can't tell me how, but do you do it a lot?" asked Jacob, missing Blake's show and tell hint.

"Two or three times a day. It makes your thing bigger."

"Yours must be huge then," Jacob tried to sound normal, whatever that meant when two boys talked about their dicks and how they played with them.

"It's about yea big," Blake put his hands up like a goal post. They looked far apart, farther than Jacob would've put his hands were he being honest.

"Guess your method works because that looks really big."

"So you do it the regular way, like this?" Blake made a circle with his hand and moved it up and down over his crotch.

"Yeah, so what?" challenged Jacob.

"Okay, I'll show you how I do it. You spit in your palms and rub the head between your hands until you cum." Blake put his hands between his legs and rubbed back and forth as if he were starting a fire with sticks.

An intensity overcame Jacob, as if a wave of hormones rushed over some breakwater, protecting him from being swept out to a depth where he would have no control. But how to translate any of this talk into action?

"Back to the game. Now that the guards are dead, what do you suggest I do Master?"

"I'd go rescue the girl. The question is, what are you going to do?" Blake slapped his inner thighs. His half-smile curled into a challenge.

Jacob had grown tired of the Dungeons and Dragons. Tired of roleplaying. "I find the Chieftain and use the Charm Person spell to make him like me."

"Here's the saving throw," said Blake, taking his time to properly (and suggestively) shake the dice. "Good job. He likes you. A lot."

"Then I ask him to let the Mayor's daughter return safely with me."

"The problem is, he likes you all right," said Blake. "But he doesn't have to do what you say."

"I'm prepared for that scenario," said Jacob.

"Well, Mr. Clever, what is your plan?"

"I tell him to come to the graveyard with the Mayor's daughter after the clock strikes midnight. There, I'll give him treasure far more valuable than the girl. If the treasure pleases him, he must let her go."

"The Chieftain is intrigued. He will meet you." Blake sat back and crossed his arms. "You're better at this than last year. How did that happen?"

"I found some D & D nerds at school. They gave me tips."

"Nerds?"

"Sure. Everyone's in a clique. I'm a band fag."

"Or maybe just a fag," teased Blake. "The clock is about to strike midnight. The moon is hidden behind threatening gray clouds. A fog rolls across the graves. Suddenly, the Chieftain steps into view with the daughter."

"And I, Orthanach, have strategically hidden all the village men behind the trees and the tombstones. They jump out with pitchforks and spears and threaten to kill the Chieftain if he doesn't release the daughter."

Blake laughed. "I get it. You want to do something else. Okay, the daughter goes free, but the Chieftain escapes into the fog."

Later that evening, Jacob broke his promise to Blake as soon as he could get to the bathroom. He let out all his frustration, repeating Blake's words: "rub the head" and "cum" until Jacob did. ☙

CHAPTER XIV

Fitted for Destruction

There was no time for sleep inertia. The entire household had to be up and ready: Jacob had to catch the bus at five after seven to get to his new school. Seventh grade had already started, and his anxiety about being the new kid turned loose his Obsessive Compulsive Disorder with enthusiasm. He checked his pimples in the mirror three or four times. He applied and reapplied Clearasil to cover up the angry red ones. Before he left, he checked the locks on the doors not once, not twice, but three times.

Click teeth. Nod. Odd numbers counteract the bad. Everything is fine.

The dread of the day settled into his body. He dragged himself to the bus stop shuffling his legs as if sandbags had been tied around his ankles. A group of older boys huddled together like vultures surrounding carrion. They made furtive side glances and mumbled as he approached. Jacob stood several feet from the wake. He said nothing but gave a nod. More snickers. He wished he had a prop to appear busy, such as a book or his Walkman. With every gear grind and rumble from a diesel engine, he whipped his neck in the boys' direction and scanned the road for the school bus.

Finally, it came. He would let them get on first, out of deference. He prayed to find a seat by himself.

Melody was refusing to take the bus—of course she was—and Rose wasn't going to push, she would get her to the new elementary school by eight-thirty.

It was Edwin's first day at Masi Furniture as a salesman. He had to drive forty-five minutes to Bradenton; it was a long drive, the gas money would be a drain on the budget, but he told Rose the opportunity to work for such a prestigious furniture store was rare, and he had his sights on a management position. Rose liked the idea of getting a discount on new furniture.

Once she had everyone else taken care of, Rose could get back to work unpacking boxes and decorating the living room. With the sale of the furniture store and their house in Pierceville, the Murtaughs were able to build a new home in Rich Valley, a growing suburb outside of Tampa. Faith had been paid off, and there were no hard feelings between Paul and Edwin (Paul and his wife were having marital trouble, therefore staying in Long Island would be best). Both sets of grandparents were now only twenty minutes away, a good distance. Like Neapolitan ice cream, Rich Valley was an option with flavors that pleased the entire family, even the one with the pickiest appetite.

The subdivision was like a sunny island, where

tranquility ruled the sidewalk, and new homes mixed old and young couples. An island blessed by God with little traffic.

The Murtaugh's built on a cul-de-sac which hadn't existed months before. It had been a privately owned citrus grove. Edwin was careful to mark a few trees he wanted the contractors to leave. Now the Murtaughs could enjoy fresh grapefruit and oranges every morning for breakfast if only someone in the family had the ambition to pick, squeeze, and section the fruit.

Rose didn't like how far the kids had to be bused, but there was a large grocery store and a Lutheran church just up the road. She had her reservations about it though because the pastors were husband and wife, and a woman wearing the white collar behind the pulpit was a little much for Rose Murtaugh. She didn't mind women leading the youth group, that was a position she had herself enjoyed and would probably volunteer for at Messiah Lutheran, assuming she could stomach the female pastor.

Rich Valley was a city they could grow into, Rose thought, challenges and all.

One of the boys from the bus stop turned around. "So new kid, you ever been neck-up in pussy before? Or are you a faggot?"

Jacob froze. Why did kids talk this way? he wondered. How should he answer? "No to both," said Jacob, bowing his head then feeling angry about his nonresistance. His face burned.

"What, your mama didn't give birth to you?" All the kids within earshot laughed.

"The new kid's an alien," chanted one boy.

"And a faggot. He's never had pussy," another chimed in. When insulted, Jacob's mind caught like a stuck clutch. Ignoring the boys' taunts and pretending he was thick-skinned would only invite more jeers. He needed to learn smart comebacks. He had to crush them with his words like Axler could.

Jacob stepped off the bus at Rich Valley Middle School. Most of the brick buildings were coated with thick, white paint. The rooftops were covered in reddish-orange shingles. They seemed like Spanish military barracks. Kids with Walkmans and book bags crisscrossed in front of him, darting to their classes. Parachute pants swished, and charm bracelets jingled. He wore the right garb on the outside but was all wrong on the inside.

You're the only one who doesn't know where to go. He walked along the sidewalk to the main office. He had no schedule, no books, no friends.

You don't belong here. He imagined stepping into first period to face the kids and their taunts: Where did you come from? What makes you think you get to be here? We were here first.

Just as his stomach twisted around like a hot coil, tempting him to retreat to the space behind his eyes, an idea came to him. *What would happen if I acted like Rue?* He was in a new place and had no allegiance to his former self or ways of doing things.

"If you can pretend it, you can master it," Axler had told him.

He stood up straight and imagined how his voice would sound if he spoke with Rue's rhythm and tonality. Before entering the administration office, he visualized Rue walking in front of him. She stops. Jacob strips away all the feminine parts of her movements. What remains is an eidolon confident, socially adroit, curious, alert; everything he was not. Using a technique he'd learned from his sessions with Rue, he steps into her image and walks in her footsteps. Her voice becomes his voice, her resources open to him.

Jacob used this visual "hit" of Rue like taking a toke on a joint. If he felt his mood slip, he imagined her, heard her voice, brought himself into the hologram, and became her.

He opened the glass door to the administration office and strode toward the secretary. Only her shiny purple-gray hair crowned the high counter.

"Good morning, I'm Jacob Murtaugh. This is my first day at Rich Valley and—"

A sour face looked up at him. "Sit down in the chair, and I'll call you when it's your turn." Her nose and lips puckered like fabric along a seam.

Before Quantum Change, a reaction like this would have crushed Jacob; would have stopped him in his tracks. Without question, he would have sat down in the chair. But he didn't feel like sitting down. He wanted his schedule so he could get to class before the bell.

"Well, look at that," said Jacob, "I do believe you dropped your—" he paused and stretched his hand down towards her desk and pointed his finger. The secretary stopped writing, looked at his finger, and followed it as he slowly raised it up to his mouth. "—smile," he said, showing off his canines. She grinned. "People say I have vampire teeth," Jacob pointed to each one, "but I prefer to think of them like werewolf fangs." He growled through a smile.

"You're adorable. What did you say your name was?"

He got his schedule and made a friend. Old Alice Morton couldn't stand any other kid in that school, but she had a soft spot for Jacob Murtaugh until the day he left.

Jacob took another toke off Rue as he made his way to English, but the closer he came to the room, the harder it was to hold on to her.

By the time he reached Mrs. McMann's class, he was nearly stuttering his name. She pointed to a seat. It was in the back corner near a window, which he was thankful for; he could watch the other kids in class and gauge their personalities, plus he had a view of the students walking to class outside. He was like a sniper-profiler, observing his classmates. He noticed their subtle tells that revealed their personality and stored them in his memory for later use when he needed to placate, leverage, or persuade.

Mrs. MacMann closed the door. All the seats were filled. The green walls mixed with sunlight washed the air in a yellow-lime glow. Jacob noticed a dark-skinned boy with wavy black hair. He had seen him at church with his family. They always sat on the other side. Jacob had not spoken to him before, for he was unsure if the boy spoke English. He never came to Sunday school or other youth events, which made Jacob suspicious.

Jacob's father said the family had moved from Lebanon.

"Aren't terrorists in Lebanon?" Jacob asked.

"There are terrorists everywhere, but especially the Middle East," said Edwin. "But there are also Arab Christians there, and this boy's family must be some of them."

Jacob studied the back of the boy's head. His neck was tan and slender. When he finally turned around to pass back dittos, Jacob flapped a hand meaning, *I've seen you before.* The boy waved with a surprised look of recognition, glad to see Jacob; almost relieved. Or maybe that was Jacob's own feeling. He wanted to write the boy a note: What's your name? When did you come to America? When is your lunch? Will you be my friend forever? But he knew a note wasn't the best approach. Girls passed notes to boys they liked. In a different world, Jacob would too.

He'd catch the boy after class and walk with him.

Klaus hacked the soft ground with the same iron hoe his father used to tear up the earth at the Ramburg homestead outside of Donalsonville, Georgia. The ground needed to be cleared before the rain started. He gripped the old, smooth hickory handle and took another whack.

Audrey stuck her head out the back door. "Klaus... Klaus, I'm goin' on, I'll see you there later." She set a cold glass of lemonade on the steps and watched him rip at the earth.

"Okay," was all he said, never looking up. Audrey disappeared into the house.

They were to celebrate her sister's fiftieth wedding anniversary. For months, Audrey had been planning with her other sisters, Donald's wife Gina, and Rose. Klaus wanted to show up and get it over with. Large, heavy raindrops hastened his pace. By the time the plot of land for his peanut crop was in outline, he was drenched. He put the tools in the shed and went in to get ready.

Klaus stepped out of the shower in the white bathroom; he wrapped his towel around his toned waist; he plugged in his Remington electric shaver; he buzzed the light gray and white stubble away. Men with beards can't be trusted, he told himself. He'd known this from his army days. They always have something to hide, that type.

He splashed aftershave on his face and his bald head. He pulled up his white boxer briefs, buttoned up his yellow starched shirt (still warm from Audrey's iron), and put on his brown suit. She had picked out a golden tie for him, but he put it back. He preferred the slate blue with silver dots. She'll gripe, but he would wear it anyway. He slid into his well-polished, plain brown leather loafers, grabbed the keys to his remodeled 1950 Ford F1 pickup, climbed into the green cab, and puttered off to the celebration.

He kept the radio off. He didn't listen to music unless he was with Audrey. *Music is noise that deafens a man to his own thoughts.* The rubber wipers slapped the rain like a drummer beating out a march. He preferred to drive without Audrey. "A man can't think when there's a woman always yapping," he said out loud. But you had to respect a man and a woman with fifty years of marriage like Fred and Liora, he thought. And they loved the Lord, too, like he did; they were good Baptist people. Fred was a deacon. Wherever he went, he passed out pamphlets proclaiming the salvation of Jesus and detailed God's Plan For Mankind. He saved lots of souls. More than Klaus.

Klaus wondered if their pretty little granddaughter, Christie, would be there. He liked to have her sit on his lap.

Please don't let me get caught, he prayed.

After the party, when the Ramburgs arrived home, firetrucks were spraying white streams of water through the blackened windows and into the gaping hole in the roof near the back. Red and blue hazard lights blinked and flashed on the tall cedars along the gravel driveway, like overgrown Christmas trees on display. The sky was orange and smokey. Blazing embers took flight like Hell-crickets.

Audrey tried to run inside, but Klaus grabbed her arm. She was screaming about Rose's cedar chest, the family's silver, the photos, her jewelry. Edwin and Rose were talking with the fire chief. Jacob and Melody sat in the van, tears streamed down their faces. *What did it mean to lose everything you owned? Was any of it going to be saved?* Jacob's thoughts spiraled out of control. There was nowhere safe to avert his eyes to click and nod. The bad was everywhere. He shut his eyelids and tried to imagine his home in Rich Valley, safe and protected. *Click teeth and nod:* a fire broke out in his bedroom. *Click teeth, nod:* a thief waiting behind a door. He pressed his fingers into his eyes until the bright silver sparkles gave him a vague image of his house being safe: *Click teeth and nod. Locked in.*

"You're a freak," Melody said. "What are you doing?"

"It's just a thing. I can't help it. Leave me alone."

Donald held his mother. Klaus squinted as the orange and red blaze flashed high into the air, scorching some of the pine branches. The fire chief told Rose the hole in the roof had been caused by a lightning bolt when it struck the white bathroom shower.

Daddy barely escaped, she thought. She looked at him with astonishing pity. His figure, which before had towered over her, appeared diminished, suppressed against the backdrop of his burning home. "It's like God tried to get him," Rose told Edwin as they were driving back to Rich Valley.

"Rose, you don't believe that, do you?" Of course she believed that, he thought. In her mind, everything is a tool for revenge—even God.

Thinking Melody and Jacob were asleep she said, "How else do you explain the shower getting struck when he'd just been in it?"

"If it was a punishment, then God missed."

"I didn't say it was a punishment. But for what Daddy might have done to Melody and to me, maybe it was a wake-up call."

"Might have done, Rose? You don't believe our daughter?"

"Something may have happened, but she does exaggerate. You know that."

"Rue seems to think—"

"Rue will say whatever she needs to take our money. It all comes down to money. How are Mama and Daddy gonna rebuild that beautiful house?"

"They have good insurance. I'm sure they'll build right over the ruins."

"They will if Mama has her way. But it'll take a while. Wonder where they'll stay."

"They're not staying with us," said Edwin.

"If it was your parents they would."

"My father hasn't touched our daughter."

"That's not even why, and you know it. You just don't like them."

"What's to like, Rose? When I asked for your father's blessing to marry you he said, 'Not on my life. You're a Catholic, and that makes you as good a nigger.'"

"But he's changed. They both have. They love you like a son."

"I don't get you. One minute you're sure God is out to teach him a lesson, and the next you want to nominate him for sainthood."

"My daddy almost got killed, Edwin. And I'm a victim, too. Have a little compassion. You don't understand; you were born with a silver spoon in your hand and with perfect parents."

"Perfect parents? My father was no monster, but I was constantly compared to Tommy. Nothing I could do would ever please Dad because Tommy did it better. But I wouldn't call myself a victim."

Jacob heard the animosity in their voices. They were like birds in a jungle chirping and cawing at cross purposes. Neither could listen to the other because they were more concerned with defending their territory. He wished they would learn from Rue. They could get better, he told himself. But all the opportunity Rue had to offer them was wasted, like all that water on the flames of his grandparents' house.

"The fire certainly was significant, Jacob, but I don't believe God caused it. I do, however believe people bring things into their lives."

"You mean Grandaddy caused it?" Jacob asked.

"It's possible to attract what we need to change us. Ram Dass taught, 'Everything is a vehicle for transformation.' I can't think of anything more transformational than a lightning bolt through the shower," Rue slapped her thighs and cackled. Then she looked out the large glass window and let the dark river carry away her thoughts except for one, "Your mother is in so much denial around her father; she's putting Melody at risk." The timbre of her voice matched the profundity of both the danger of the situation and the wild black-green current flowing just outside the door.

"What can we do?"

Rue lifted her hands in the air. "Pray."

"But we have to own our thoughts because our thoughts become reality; you taught me that," said Jacob.

"It's true. You must own your own thoughts. But you can't own someone else's. Have you heard the saying, 'You can pick your friends. You can pick your nose. But you can't pick your friend's nose?'"

"Yuck. I get it. What if praying doesn't work?"

"Then we get confrontational."

"So there is something under my control that's been bothering me. I can't seem to hold on to my resource state when I get nervous at school."

"What stops you?" Rue asked.

"I think about the kids not liking me. I think they're going to reject me."

"And you sound about three-years-old as you say that, love. It's because your mother seduced you then castrated you. It's time we get you in front of Axler to put your balls back on. Do you feel ready?"

"Seduced me? Gross!"

"It's how she moves through the world to get what she wants. To a young boy, her world was an entertaining play, and you were the star actor. There was comedy, terror, drama. She used you. Mesmerized you. Does that resonate?"

"It does," said Jacob, grabbing his stomach to keep the heaving threats from becoming a reality.

"So are you ready?"

"I am."

"Then you'll come with me to the next seminar. Are you staying with the Ramburgs at all in that trailer?"

"Hell no, Rue."

While the Ramburgs' house was being rebuilt, they lived in a trailer next door at Crawley's trailer park. Audrey's specifications were exacting. She had Klaus give the contractors the original floor plans; everything was to be recreated. The texture on the ceiling in each room must be as it was. The color of paint in the blue room and the purple room had to be the same hue as before. The palette and patterns of tile in the white and brown bathrooms

183

should be the same. The carpeting had to come from the same manufacturer; it must be swirled and plush. The counters, white laminate with gold-flecks. The linoleum must match as closely as possible. Every day she walked through the house to inspect and make a list of items that seemed askance.

One day she went into town for her beauty appointment. Klaus was watching Melody (for Rose had convinced herself and Edwin that Melody had misremembered and that the family must stick together). "Let's go over to the hay barn," he told her.

They walked to the pasture behind the house. He stepped on a muddy tire next to a fence post and climbed over the barbed-wire fence. The heifers and steers tread their way from the back pasture toward the barn, mooing expectantly. Klaus held the lowest wire for Melody to crawl under. A dragonfly landed on his boot. She stopped moving.

"Get on in here," he said.

"I'm scared of the bug, Boo Boo."

"You better get through before I let this wire go."

She swatted at the dragonfly, which zoomed and landed near the water trough, then she scrambled under the wire.

In the barn, he had her get some feed for the cows. After they fed and watered them, he brought her back into the barn to show her his collection of old glass telephone insulators he'd picked up working on the railroad. He told her she could have one, "if she was real good." Melody knew what was coming. She knew "real good" meant she had to lay in the hay with her pants down and let him rub her.

"Lay down on your belly," said Klaus. The dragonfly settled on a hay stalk. "Open your legs." She blew at it. The dragonfly hovered and settled again, agitating its wings. "You be quiet now," said Klaus. The dragonfly turned and faced her; she tried not to scream, but when Klaus inserted the hot, rough metal rod inside her, she shrieked. The dragonfly flew away. Melody thought of the mama and the baby cows and how much that mama must love her calf, to be with that baby all the time, even when it's dark and cold. She thought if she ever had a baby, she'd be like that mama calf. Klaus covered her mouth and pushed the rod further in.

Later that evening when it was bath time, Audrey cleaned her up as best she could so the tearing wouldn't show.

Rue and Jacob checked into the Tampa Hilton late Thursday afternoon. Raymond Axler would be presenting alone because Dr. Miller was giving a seminar in another country. The two men hadn't been seen together in some time. There were rumors of a spilt. But Jacob liked Axler the most; he was radical, said what he wanted, used words like, "fuck" and told dirty jokes. He said things people were thinking but were too frightened to say; at least that's what he said he was doing, and Jacob believed him.

"Will I get to meet him?" Jacob asked.

"Meet him? You're the youngest attendee here. He damn sure better pick you to come up on stage for a demonstration," said Rue.

Jacob had fantasized about sitting with Rue and Raymond Axler at a cozy hotel bar, speaking about important things such as the reluctance of American psychotherapists to use Quantum Change because it worked so well (they wouldn't be able to keep charging the same clients); yes, the success of the methodology among laymen was something to celebrate. Perhaps Rue and Raymond would banter, nearly flirt, before Raymond throws a barb, putting Rue on defense. What was it that kept Rue from remarrying? Jacob wondered.

As if to distract him from his inquiry, Rue asked, "What issue will you work on, love?" It was important to have at least one outcome in mind when one appears before Axler, she had told him.

"Any suggestions?" asked Jacob.

"How about your father?"

Was it so obvious? Wasn't it a cliche? For his own pride, he should at least pretend to have a more profound goal; to help, to heal others, so that people would think, "What an amazing boy that Jacob Murtaugh!" Axler would see through the sham. Jacob did not feel set back, but his fantasies put him on alert to his pettiness. He set his mind to work on freeing himself from his parents' insanity. There, that was real. And if his goal garnered Axler's interest in him, then all the better. He desired to come out of this workshop with an invitation to be his apprentice.

That evening, they picked up their name tags. Rue found two seats in the large conference room. "These seats are prime real estate," she told Jacob. "When he comes in, he'll walk in from the back, he always does, then he'll come straight up the aisle. I'll stand up, and he'll stop. Then I'll introduce you."

Jacob hoped her plan would work. He wiped his palms on his slacks.

"There he is," she said clapping, smiling, like everyone else. The conference lights were blaring. People were on their feet as if the President had been announced.

When Raymond brushed Rue, she grabbed his arm. "Were you going to say hello, Raymond?"

"We've got all weekend, darlin'," he said, waving across the room.

"Raymond, I want you to meet my protege." Rue took Raymond's hand.

"Protege? You're not old enough to have a protege, are you?"

"I am when he's only thirteen-years-old. This is Jacob Murtaugh."

Raymond grasped Jacob's hand. "Thirteen, eh? And you understand all this stuff?"

"Yes, sir. It's saving my life."

Raymond met Rue's eyes, and she nodded her head. "And he's damn good. Prodigy might be a better word. He'll surpass you one day, Raymond."

"You'll have to tell me all about him later tonight." Axler sauntered towards the stage.

Jacob was electrified. Rue gave him a fist bump. "We've done it, Jacob. Now keep your shit about you, work hard in the seminar tonight, and we'll see what happens."

When the hotel bartender objected to Jacob, Axler simply said, "He's with me." It was like watching Obi-Wan Kenobi wave away Stormtroopers. Jacob observed

Raymond mirroring everyone around him. When he spoke to the woman across from him, he tilted his head at the same angle she did; to the man next to him, he slowed his speech to match the man's vocal rhythm; with the bartender (he had been little more aggressive), he swung his bar stool in time with the man's breathing as he matched his visual manner of speaking. All of it was child's play for Raymond Axler.

"I do it too, what you're doing. It's better than being bored," said Jacob.

"You noticed. I'm impressed," said Axler.

"But I can't take control of as many people as you can yet."

"Take control? Rue, what are you teaching this boy? Do we have a little Hitler over here?"

Jacob's ballooning ego burst and crashed. He tried to find cover by slurping his soda.

"Is that what you think is going on, Jacob?" asked Axler.

Rue wasn't going to rescue him.

"That's kinda what it looks like," said Jacob.

"That's only what you see, kid. Having rapport with people is a dance. If I mirror your breathing, am I breathing with you or are you breathing with me?"

Jacob's eyes widened.

Axler sipped his bourbon. "It's good you brought him to me so young, Rue. Maybe we can fix some of our mistakes."

Dizzy and worn out, Jacob returned home from the seminar. He was resentful of his parents and their questions, "How was it?" "Did you learn a lot?" "What did you work on?" "What was Axler like?" Rose wanted her own therapy session. Edwin tried to reconnect out of fear. Had Axler pulled back the curtain on his flaws (as if they had been so well hidden) and turned Jacob against him? And Rose from selfishness, for anything Jacob learned she could absorb vicariously and do it just as well. She would show Rue how healthy she was; she could talk like them, use the big words, and act impressed with what Axler could do.

Jacob dropped his suitcase and laid in his bed. Axler's face floated in front of him, looming. He wanted to be like him. He never thought that about his father; there was nothing Edwin ever said or did that Jacob wanted to emulate.

Axler was more like a father, and Rue a mother. He could see this idea forming in his mind before he understood it. Images of his parents paraded before him, then blurred and faded, as a water-logged photograph becomes flimsy and anemic. They were to him like dangerous people he loved and had to protect (from themselves), not sources of wisdom.

But how can a son trade out his parents? wondered Jacob, shocked at the insincerity of the question. He gazed at the brown ceiling fan and defocused his eyes until the blades appeared to coalesce into a transparent wheel. I see through them, through the emptiness of their lives, the hollowness of their being. The more he thought of Rue and Axler, the more he sensed being free of his parents, from everything like them. He was not aware of the chill from the breeze in the air. It was the cold nerve of surety that jolted him from being transfixed on the choice he must make.

But what about Melody? He wished she could understand Edwin and Rose's failure. She continually reached out for her mother, but Rose was incapable of giving back. One's concern or problem became engulfed in her bottomless need for attention and devotion. She had eaten her twin in her mother's womb and would consume anyone who came to close to her; and Edwin didn't have the strength to stop her.

Was it self-preservation? Was it pride? Was it, again, the hope of reconciliation, such that all the warning signs, bitter as Wormwood to anyone else, were concealed in the saccharine duty of loyalty? Or were they suppressed by the shame of one's own missteps, which were many in the Murtaugh family? When Rose discovered Klaus had abused Melody again, her failure to protect her daughter triggered more of her own abuse memories, which took front and center.

Sitting on Rue's couch with her arms around Rose's neck, weeping at the thought that her mother would never be able to set aside her own suffering, Melody imagined how in the chambers of her mother's heart, who was shivering and shaking next to her, were boxes wrapped in shiny paper and bows, arranged like gifts around a Christmas tree, which if she could open them, they would transmit everything a daughter needs from a mother, but they would never be given to her freely. By what device, either love or trauma, could she unwrap those gifts in her mother's heart? How could the two of them merge, like rivers running along a watershed into the same lake? For it was not gifts nor understanding she craved, but a mother's heartfelt acceptance.

And yet, nothing came from Rose. She was a dry river bed. She wondered how it was possible to perceive her daughter's needs and not provide for them. How could she be so cold as to murder her own maternal stirrings? Rose broke loose from her daughter and stood. She walked over to Rue and crumpled on the floor, wrapping her arms around Rue's legs.

"Mama," she cried.

Melody walked outside. She found Jacob sitting on the dock, tossing acorns in the river.

"What's wrong with our parents?" Melody asked.

"What parents? We're orphans."

Rue pushed for a confrontation with the Ramburgs before they left for the mountains. Rose finally relented. But Klaus and Audrey would only agree to meet if a mediator of their choosing, a Christian mediator, also attended. Reverend Lloyd King, Klaus' longtime friend and best man at his wedding (his wife Beatrice was Audrey's Maid of Honor), agreed to assist with the intervention.

Melody sat on a swing on the porch overlooking the river. It flowed like liquid obsidian. Inside Rue's condo, Edwin and Rose sat next to Lloyd on the plush L-shaped sectional that bent around the living room. Rue paced back and forth in front of Klaus interrogating him, unintimidated by the Baptist deacon and the decorated war veteran sitting with his arms crossed, steely-eyed in his chair, unflinching, as if to say, "Hit me."

"A little girl, Mr. Ramburg. A tiny little girl. You tore her open so badly she has scars," Rue said in her opening. "What in God's name do you have to say for yourself?"

"I didn't mean to hurt her, Mrs. Pedersen."

"Did you touch her, Mr. Ramsburg?" asked Rue.

"I let her sit on my lap. She touched me, and I touched her a little bit."

"Now, Klaus, you need to tell the truth. You're the adult here," said Lloyd.

"I only touched her a little bit."

Rue folded her arms and walked closer to look into his face. "And what do you call that, Mr. Ramburg?" He shifted in his chair.

"I'm sorry for what I done. God has forgiven me."

"What makes you so sure, Mr. Ramburg? There's a little girl in the next room who needs to hear you say you're sorry. There's a family that has been through Hell because of what you've done to that little girl, and probably to others. What do you call that damage, Mr. Ramburg?"

"He said he was sorry," Audrey defended through clenched teeth, gripping Klaus' arms. "I don't know what kind of woman you are talking to a man like this, but we have words for people like you where I come from; words I can't say here in front of a man of God."

Rue smiled. "Audrey, where I come from, we have a word for women who cover up the sins of men like Klaus and stand behind them. We call those women pedophiles. And we have places for them just like their men—jail."

"We don't have to sit here and take this," Audrey shrieked. "Klaus get in the car. If you want to let this woman tear your family apart you go ahead, Rose, but mark my words, this is an evil woman, and no good will come from this. He's said he's sorry, now we need to move on."

When they left, Lloyd sighed and slumped back into the chair. "I'm afraid that's the best you can hope for from those two," he said, "You'll probably never hear any more from them about this."

"Reverend King, when we brought this up to you, why were you so quick to believe Klaus could have molested Melody?" asked Rue.

"Because he's a sexual pervert. I've known that about him since he got married, and he and Audrey came back early from their honeymoon. Audrey come to my wife a bloody mess on account of that monster."

"I think he's done things to me too, Brother Lloyd," said Rose.

"I wouldn't doubt it, child. And I worry for Carol Alice and Lena, and all the little girls in this family."

Rue walked to the center of the room. "Melody won't be getting an apology today, people. But she got her admission. We have that success to bring her. How we frame that is essential to her healing."

Rue brought Melody in. She sat down next to her mother, who brushed her hair with her fingers, out of her own need of self-comfort. Rose's eyes were wet and red. Melody had long tired of the scene because she knew Rose only cried for herself. She went cold inside each time Rose's hand touched her. Edwin put his arm around Melody in a chummy way; he lacked the mental presence and emotional center to sense her agitation and to extend himself into it to calm her. She needed an anchor to hold her somewhere safe.

"Melody, today was a win, love. For you, for your mom, for young girls who are survivors all over. We didn't get everything, but we got a lot considering what a tough nut to crack that man is." Melody relaxed her spine and leaned into the couch. Rose mistook the movement as Melody drawing close. As soon as Rose leaned closer, Melody stiffened up again.

"He confessed. He didn't give details. He said he was sorry, but as we all know, it's the kind of sorry typical of criminal thinkers—he's sorry he got caught," said Rue. "But dammit, he admitted he did it."

Melody began to cry. She had not made up the story, like Rose wanted to believe, like the cousins wanted to say, like the voices whispered to her when she was in her bed and couldn't sleep, afraid to remember, afraid to forget.

"What are we going to do now?" she asked Rue.

"Your mother needs to call the police and make a report."

"The police?" repeated Rose. She moved away from Melody. "But he confessed. What good will calling the police do?"

"He's a baby-fucker and needs to be in jail. That's what the police will do, God-dammit," said Rue.

Edwin burst out laughing. The truth, when spoken so plainly, undecorated, unmoderated, can free emotions locked by language and pretense. Rue named what the man was; she pulled off the disguise, she unveiled the ugly, unvarnished facades of a private life and without ceremony prescribed the takedown of what had been a figure of power: Rose's father, the deacon, the World War II soldier, the patriarch, the husband, the railroad man, the grandfather, the baby-fucker. For the first time, Edwin was intimidated by Rue.

"I can't do it. I can't turn my daddy in," said Rose. For she believed he was still the amulet against Audrey, a danger she feared more than any destruction Klaus could bring to her daughter.

Just as the Ramburgs finished packing for Maggie Valley, and before Rue could persuade Rose to file a report with the police, Klaus Ramburg suffered a major heart attack.

"Was this another warning from God?" Edwin asked, pulling into the hospital parking lot.

"I've prayed on it, and God is giving him another chance," said Rose. "Maybe he's truly sorry, Edwin."

"Well, I'm not going in to see the man."

"I'll go with you, Mom," said Jacob.

Donald stopped Rose and Jacob at the door to Klaus' hospital room. Audrey pulled the green privacy curtain around the bed.

"Now's not a good time to visit," said Donald.

"I want to see my daddy," said Rose, trying to push him aside.

"Ya'll have caused enough trouble makin' up lies and havin' daddy meet with that woman. You put him in here." Donald pressed her shoulder so that she had to take a step back.

Jacob wanted to force his way past Donald and speak on behalf of his mother, on behalf of his sister, on behalf of Rue and say, "You idiots. You're protecting the wrong person!" Then he would look at Klaus and wish for God to have mercy on him. But he knew not to speak, for the primacy of belief surpassed reality. Words rarely struck their target. The padded sensations in his brain nauseated him. His powerlessness disgusted him.

Nobody will ever listen to you, said The Voice.

Suddenly, a nurse pushing an empty bed, the severe white lights in the hall, the chill of the air, the well-wishing balloon bobbing up and down attached to the running child, became like a cyclone whirling around a sinister eye, hollow and deadly.

Jacob took Rose by the hand. "Mom, let's leave."

Warm tears filled Rose's eyes which, without untangling her snarled mouth, made the air salty, ran over her cheek and clung to her chin. She had better leave before she lost control, she thought.

There would be no family vacation that summer. Jacob wrote Blake explaining he wouldn't be able to seem him. Blake wrote back:

> Jay,
>
> *I'm sorry to hear about your Grandaddy and that you can't come up to the mountains. I'll miss you so much.*
>
> *My grandparents might come down later in the year. Maybe I can come with them. If not, I hope I can see you next year.*

All my love,
Blake

P.S. Tell your mom and pops and sis hi!

Allowed at last to visit her father, still recovering in the hospital, Rose flipped through a glossy magazine in silence. Klaus watched a Western on the television. He did not speak. No one spoke. A nurse came in and wrote down numbers; she changed the saline bag; she waddled out of the room. Rose flipped a page and looked at her father. He turned up the volume with the remote. Gunfire and horse hooves drowned out the horrid emptiness. Rose flipped another page. Klaus knew, with every page turn, Rose was reminding him she was there; she pitied him. Yes—she still honored him.

The days were like that then, swallowed in the heat and the yellow air. There was Jacob, marching with his father's clarinet at summer camp. There was Melody, slender and light, practicing the Plié and Battement tendu in front of the mirrors in the studio. There was Edwin, eager and giddy, impressing bosses. Everyone was busy; everyone was dreaming; everyone was passing time.

The newness of the school year injected a freshness into the hot August month (Jacob was now in the eighth grade, and Melody in the third). But no assiduity on

Rose's part took her mind off her guilt and fear of the changes happening around her family. Jacob's social life seemed to take him away from her. Every evening he had long conversations on the phone with friends; conversations that sounded more like therapy sessions than kids hanging out, thought Rose.

"I don't like it, Rue. And I don't like you encouraging him; he's not a counselor. He's a teenage boy."

"What do you expect? He's gifted. People are naturally drawn to him. Plus, he's looking for ways to practice the techniques he's learning. What are you really concerned about, Rose?"

"These girls call every night, but he never dates. He doesn't have a girlfriend. He's helping them with their boy troubles."

"And you're wondering if there's something wrong with him."

"Other boys don't act this way. They go to movies with their girlfriends; they hold hands; Jacob shows no interest."

"I can't blame him when his mother is breathing down his neck. Give him space, Rose. Give him time."

Preparing for their Thanksgiving guests, Rose was cleaning the children's bathroom. Thomas Sr. and Elaine were coming this year. She heard the phone ring across the house. She ignored it. "If it's important, they'll call back," she said, giving the toilet bowl one last swipe.

From the kitchen, she saw the red light blinking on the answering machine. She pressed play. It was Wayne

Graf: "Rose, this is Wayne. I have some bad news to stuff in your turkey. Gimme a call." She stopped everything and dialed his number. He had contracted AIDS. She hadn't heard much about the disease other than the gays were catching it, and it was killing all their friends. He didn't think he'd beat it, he said, and made her promise to come visit him before he died.

When Jacob came home, she told him to sit on her bed. "Jacob, Wayne is dying. He has AIDS." Jacob had learned about the disease in health class. Is he being treated? Jacob wanted to know. Would she go visit him? Did he have anyone he was close to?

Rose only cried. "He can't leave me. He was the one person who showed me who I really am."

Jacob cried too. He cried for Wayne, for getting something so terrible, for being who he was. He cried because he knew he'd never see him again and wondered if he'd be able to talk to anyone again about what he did that day in Wayne's kitchen. He cried because of death. Besides a few of the older people in his extended family, its shadow had not passed by so closely.

Jacob and Raafe, his Lebanese friend from church (everyone called him Ralph), stood out in the courtyard of Rich Valley middle school after lunch on a bright blue January day. The bite in the air was already cold enough for sweaters and coats.

Jacob never missed a shuttle launch. Since Columbia, he'd caught them on television, but on this day, he joined the throng of students outside so he could look to the skies to see something unique—a teacher was going to space. The large plume cloud and fleece-colored smoke trails were wrong. He panicked, like when the news of death arrives. Nothing to do. Nowhere to go. Just be with the news. People were running inside to see it on television, but Jacob didn't. He knew they were dead.

Jacob finished school the day the Challenger exploded as if he were a machine, conscious of some program and energy moving his body, but not present to its operation. When he came home, he found Rose glued to the news. He saw the red fireball up close. Tom Brokaw confirmed what Jacob knew. All seven astronauts were lost.

That day, Jacob learned men and women can fall from the skies. And people, speeding toward a goal, can be ripped from their trajectory and thrown down and scattered by random chance.

For Jacob, it was an era when adults fell in his eyes because they chose to press toward the weaker course, and by their integrity having failed, destroyed entire systems. It was the first time in his life when God seemed distant and small, a sham; like a little man standing on a stool, desperately trying to push all the buttons before time ran out. ❧

CHAPTER XV

Captiva

For the life of her, Rose couldn't imagine why Tommy and Linda organized a reunion at a beach resort during spring break.

"So all the family could be there, including Paul and the other cousins from New York," said Edwin.

"But Captiva Island? It's so expensive. But of course, everything has to be the best for the Murtaughs." Rose pulled down her visor and checked her make-up. *Better add more mascara.* "All this hoopla over a reunion and—"

"You'd rather a shabby pavilion by a dirty lake with an outhouse and a corncob to wipe your ass?"

"What are you talking about, Edwin?"

"Last year's Ramburg reunion your clan drove to Lakesville from all over Georgia and Florida. Your mother and Aunt Thelma cooked until they dropped. It was hot and nobody—"

"I carried food and so did Gina. We had a nice potluck."

"Nobody enjoyed it except the flies and the ants."

"You didn't enjoy it because it was simple and cheap. At least there was no smoking or drinking."

"Can we listen to a tape? Something by Michael Jackson or Journey?" asked Jacob.

Rose went on about how good it was to see so-and-so; about how shocking it was to find out her cousin remarried; and how she must get Aunt Thelma's recipe for fried chicken. Edwin's attention drifted to the scenery outside: large coastal homes with massive walls of glass offered an expansive view of the ocean; fire pits and grills on patios adorned crystal clear swimming pools; tall, swaying palm trees outlined the property. He projected himself (and only himself) inside the living room of one of those homes. He watched a football game at full volume; unable to hear Jacob, or Rose bitching about how fat she will look in her bathing suit.

"Edwin? Are you even listening?" asked Rose.

"I was thinking about something. What?"

"You're always daydreaming." Rose stared out her window, which meant, *You've offended me.* Edwin shrugged his shoulders, which meant, *It's not my problem.* Rose sighed, meaning, *You never care about my feelings.*

"Mom thinks she'll look fat in her bathing suit," informed Melody.

Edwin tried to make Rose feel better, but nothing satisfied her because her real aim was to blame him for not making enough money to make her comfortable, despite his promotion to General Manager.

And she wanted to argue, needed to argue because it helped her relax. Edwin chewed on the quick of his nails.

There will be golf matches and parties; plenty of ways to get away from her, he thought. I'll get to spend some time with my brothers, maybe play some tennis, fish, sail. After he had filled his week's schedule, he realized he hadn't planned to do anything with Jacob, one on one. He couldn't imagine Jacob would want to come golfing or fishing. He'd probably want to go see a movie, but they could do that at home. There were going to be lots of kids there; Jacob could find something to do with them.

"Does anyone want to listen to music?" asked Jacob.

Rose put on Glenn Frey. Edwin fast-forwarded the cassette to Party Town. "Remember this?" Edwin asked, smirking at Rose. Of course she did. Wayne had loved it. He had loved any song about partying because his life had been one big party. So was his funeral (he left strict orders to only play dance music at his wake).

Rose turned the music down. If Wayne were there, he'd tell her to shut up and just wear the damn yellow swimsuit even if she looked like a bruised banana. "I'm sure Linda will be dressed to the nines. She always looks like the perfect golfer's wife."

"Why do you always compete with her?" Edwin jutted out his chin. The vein in his temple began to pulse. Melody and Jacob looked at one another. They felt bad for their father.

"Will we have our own rooms?" asked Melody, trying to distract.

"You and Jacob will share a suite. Your mother and I will be right next door," said Edwin.

"Can we go swimming when we get there?"

"After we unpack." Edwin was already exhausted from

the talking.

"How does the room key thing work, Dad? It's like a credit card, right?"

"Yes, Jacob, but you're not to spend a bunch of money. You'll have a daily allowance, and once you spend that, there's no more. I'm not made of money, dammit."

"Geez, Dad. Relax. I was just asking."

"Well, I'm sorry it's not enough for us to go on a vacation. No one can be happy about that. Everybody's wanting to spend, spend, spend. I just got this new promotion. How about we save a little bit for Christ's sake."

Rose waved her hand. "It's not like you're paying for our rooms, Edwin. Tommy and your father are taking care of all that. We wouldn't be able to come if it weren't for them."

She always had to knock him down a notch. And when she became too secure, Edwin had to destabilize her life. It was part of the tension in the coil that ignited their union. When they met, it was as if their souls parleyed on behalf of each body; Rose would be the woman Edwin could disappoint because Edwin would be the boy she could destroy.

Palm trees, like thick walls, and knee-high shrubs, enclosed the resort. If not for the seagulls, the salt-spray falling on the tongue like dew, and the sound of waves crashing nearby, one might mistake the Gulf Breeze Resort parking lot and surrounds for a backlot at Disney studios. The resort buildings were white ziggurats, gleaming and bleached, sprouting like clusters of waxen fruit from the unnatural, overly fertilized green grass.

Melody and Jacob unpacked with the efficiency of worker ants in a colony, carrying more of their weight than was normally possible and at a greater speed than usual. Both children were spurned on by a common goal: to get into one of the luxurious pools. They both had their goggles and flippers, Jacob brought a snorkel, Melody a pail, shovel, and some figurines to dive for. The coconut scent of sunscreen mixed with the pungent chlorine tang in the air.

At play in the water, whether it was a beach or a pool, the environs became like tocsins for Jacob's desire. He floated his chin against the blue surface tension of the water, scanning the area. Jacob's eyes came to rest on a tan boy in a Speedo leaning against the metal rail of the steps leading into the pool.

"What is the name?" the boy called out in broken English.

"I'm Jacob. What's yours?"

His teeth, his chest, his blonde hair, his thick red lips, the bulge behind the tiny piece of blue and white wet fabric; Jacob gazed back over them as if taking inventory. He locked onto the boy's blue eyes. A drop of water escaped the boy's chin, landed below his navel, and threatened to drizzle down the bulge. Jacob's eyes tried to free themselves from their incarceration.

Drip.

Liquid soaked into the Speedo. *Keep eye contact.* The boy brushed his chest sending a cascade of pool water down his smooth belly. *Don't look.*

Too late. The boy noticed.

"I am Erik. I don't speak English good. Maybe you teach me?"

Jacob drifted, gator-like, toward Erik. "Where are you from?"

"Germany. I am here on vacation." Erik slipped into the pool and met Jacob face to face.

"I'd like to learn German. We could teach each other."

"Good. I teach you to count first," said Erik. In seconds, his slender hands grabbed Jacob's. He shaped one finger of Jacob's right hand. "*Eins*. You say." He made two fingers, "*Zwei*. Now you. *Drei*. Yah! Good accent. *Vier, Funf*." Erik held his hand against Jacob's. It was nearly the same size, but his skin was darker. "Where from you, Jacob?"

"We say, 'Where are you from,' and I'm from here. Florida."

"You like German cars? We make best."

"I'm not really into cars. I like music."

"German music best. You know *Die Toten Hosen*?"

"They're so cool," Jacob lied. "Have you ever seen them in concert?"

"Not 'cool.' We say *supergeil*! Concert? Nein. I am hungry. You come to my room. We talk about German food."

There was no one in Erik's suite. Showing no modesty, he threw his towel on the floor and took off his Speedo.

"Don't like wet feeling." His genitals dangled and swung like a bell as he walked around. He enjoyed being watched. He reached for this, bent over to pick up that.

"You also undress. No wet clothes." Jacob obeyed. Erik watched as Jacob removed his bathing suit, hesitating, holding it in front of him, then dropping it on the floor.

"Ah, *beschnitten*," he said, pointing to Jacob's penis. "How you say in English?"

208

Jacob feigned confusion. Erik came closer holding his penis in his hand, shook it, then pointed to Jacob's. "*Beschnitten*," he said again.

"Circumcised," said Jacob.

"Yah, I like." Erik laid his own on top of Jacob's penis and rubbed them. "How you say this?"

The motion of Erik's hand made Jacob lose his balance. He rested his arm on Erik's shoulder and stroked his neck, watching Erik's hand working back and forth.

"Jerking off," said Jacob.

The waves crashed outside; coconut and chlorine swirled and mixed with the new smells of boy, sand, and summer.

"So, Jacob are you having a good time in Captiva? You've hardly spent any time with your old uncle," said Tommy. "We only see you when your friend is off somewhere with his family."

"Yes, he's teaching me German. I can count now. Wanna hear? *Eins, zwei, drei, veir, funf*—"

"You better be careful with that last one. Words with f-u in them are dangerous."

Elaine laughed. Linda laughed. Edwin laughed. If Tommy made a joke, everyone had to laugh. Jacob sat stunned. Did Tommy suspect something?

"Don't worry, son. You'll understand when you're older," said Edwin.

Jacob got the joke but tried to look aggrieved to dampen any conjecture. He walked out to the balcony to sulk.

So much depends then, thought Jacob, watching

the emerald liquid heave and spit foamy white crests upon itself and suck them back in, so much depends, he thought, on impressions: no matter how well a person knows one, people form opinions too quickly; for his feeling for Erik had been overtaken, engulfed by a wave and sunk as he watched the green mass pulse; as slimy white fingers seized sand and shells ebulliently into frothy lips.

When Erik asked Jacob to spend the night, he lied and said his parents wouldn't allow it.

"*Dann schleich.*"

"*Schleich?* What's this?"

Erik put an arm around Jacob and made two fingers run across the air.

"Sneak? I can't. Melody will hear and tell."

"Oh well," said Erik. "Too bad."

All the next day, Jacob avoided him. If he saw Erik at the pool, he went to the beach. If Erik was dining, Jacob went out to a cabana. If he was in the jacuzzi, Jacob turned into the arcade.

"You are here," Erik said, pressing himself against Jacob from behind.

"Stop it. What are you doing? People are looking."

"Let's go to room."

"No. I can't now. I can't anymore. My family wants me to spend more time with them. I'm sorry."

"I don't understand. What wrong?"

"I'll see you. They're waiting for me."

The sun had set on the second to last night of the reunion.

Prince's *1999* video blared from the television. Elaine and Thomas Sr. were buzzed. Edwin was working his way to the bottom of a bottle of white wine. Rose went to bed with a migraine. The cousins were all in the pool. Jacob snuck a few pulls from a whiskey bottle then made his way out to the pool deck. His cousin Paulo swam alone in the deep end. Jacob made a cannonball entrance and paddled after the boy.

Paulo admired Jacob (he was twelve and Jacob was fourteen). The boys wrestled in the water.

"You snuck some beer," said Paulo. "Get me some."

"It's not beer. It's whiskey. I'll get you some if you do a dare."

"Depends on what it is."

"Nope. Forget it. I'll throw you across the pool instead." Jacob picked up Paulo like a wet duffle bag and tossed him further into the deep end. The other cousins, all girls, were getting splashed.

"You boys are so rowdy," one whined, and they trotted off to the jacuzzi like a harem of feral fillies.

Paulo swam to Jacob and hung on his shoulders. He wiped chlorine soaked tendrils of raven hair from his eyes. "Okay, I'll do it."

"I dare you to take off your bathing suit, dive and touch the bottom."

"That's easy," said Paulo. His firm, tan chest glistened in the white and blue pool lights. His skin was slick like a dolphin. Jacob's eyes followed the shape of his torso; his body tapered at his waist, like an arrow; his belly-button pouted like a tied balloon. Paulo got naked. His turquoise suit, covered in yellow robots sipping Pina

Coladas from coconuts, floated past Jacob. As Paulo dove to the bottom, Jacob grabbed it and threw it out of the pool. Paulo's round ass flashed palely on the surface.

A sensation came over Jacob, a remote feeling like a film or a partition had been placed between his thoughts and his actions.

"Did it! Now let me have some of that whiskey."

"Not yet. Now you have to do pull-ups on that ladder."

"Naked? Okay. But the wind will be cold."

"What, you worried about your dick shriveling up? Come here. I'll warm you up first." Paulo let Jacob put his arms around his waist and pull him close. They floated in the middle of the pool. "You don't feel very shriveled," said Jacob. The boy pushed his waist into Jacob. "You still want that whiskey?"

"Maybe. I dunno."

"Never mind the pull-ups, I'll go get us some. Put on your bathing suit."

Elaine smoked her Raleigh and sipped a mimosa under a white veranda by the pool. She worked her crossword puzzle, a daily ritual for over thirty years.

"Good morning, Jay. Help me, I'm stumped." Jacob sat down and quaffed from Elaine's mimosa. "That's not good for you dear, don't drink that."

"Neither is that cigarette, Nana." He took another gulp.

"Okay, smarty-pants. Three across, 'These always come in last place.' Middle letter is Y."

"Are you sure 'Y' is right?"

"Yes, I'm sure. 'College application parts.' It's 'essays.'"

"Remember that time I wanted to know if sharks had tongues, and I asked Mom and Dad? They didn't really know, so I told them I'd ask Nana because she knows everything." Elaine chortled like a jungle bird. Her cigarette vibrated between her tremoring fingers.

"Yes, I remember. Your old Nana knows a thing or two, but not everything."

"Jacob, let's go," Edwin called from the breezeway. The golf drag show had begun. His father wore black polyester golf slacks and a fire engine red shirt. He had on a matching visor with the name of his favorite ball emblazoned in red cursive letters across the front. A single white golf glove flashed as he walked. Dennis' ensemble was less garish: stormy gray slacks with a teal green shirt. He was the more sensible of the two and waited until they arrived at the greens to put on his hat and glove.

"The answer is X, Y ,Z. Love you." Jacob kissed Elaine on the cheek and left the veranda.

"Your Uncle Tom wants to give you a private golf lesson this morning before everyone else gets there," said Edwin.

"I don't need it, Dad. With Quantum Change, I can just watch him and model his skill. I'll pick up more that way."

"Jacob, now is not the time to talk about Quantum Change. He wants to teach you, give you some putting and driving tips. Just let him. Do you know how many kids would appreciate having a lesson from a pro-golfer like your uncle?"

"But having golf lessons by a pro is meaningful because they've assigned that meaning to it. I don't. It would be like a bum trying to force you to learn how to find food in the trash. Would that be meaningful to you?"

Jacob didn't mean to equate Thomas, Jr. to a bum or golf to trash, but that was the message both Edwin and Dennis received.

"My dad, your Papa, would have set me straight if I had talked to him that way," said Dennis.

"Jacob, keep your mouth shut and be appreciative," said Edwin.

Jacob resented his father's lack of interest in Quantum Change. He resented his recreant attitude towards his abilities. How was it possible Rue, Axler, and others in the Quantum Change community were calling him a prodigy and an example to follow, yet his father didn't have faith in his son's ability to get his uncle interested in a technology that was becoming relevant to athletes all over the world?

He had no intention of staying quiet.

"Let's start on the driving range, Jacob. I think it's been since Christmas, you were about eight when we picked up some clubs together in my front yard." Tommy was the largest of the three brothers, had a white, plastic television smile, wore a large-brim straw golf hat, Irish green slacks, and a white golf shirt.

"Actually Uncle Tommy, if you don't mind, I'd like to watch you hit a few balls and then try it myself without any pointers."

"Jacob…" Edwin threatened through gritted teeth. Jacob ignored his father.

"I've been trained in this radical psychological technology called Quantum Change. The whole thing is about how we create experience and how to reproduce excellence in the world."

"You sound like a motivational speaker." Tommy wiped beads of sweat off his forehead.

"So, yeah, I haven't really hit a golf ball in years. But how about I try a few first, then you go. I'll do my thing and try again."

"Okay, you do your thing," said Tommy. He winked at Edwin as Jacob teed up his ball.

On the first swing, Jacob's club gouged two inches of grass and dirt just in front of the ball. On the second swing, he topped the ball and sent it rolling a few feet. On the third try, he made contact but sent the golf ball flying behind him several feet.

"Okay, Uncle Tom, your turn. I'll watch."

"Should I be impressed yet?" asked Tommy.

Edwin grabbed Jacob by the arm. "I've had enough. Straighten up or I'll tell your mother you were an ass on the golf course and you'll never go to another seminar or read those Quantum books again," Edwin whispered.

"Go ahead, Dad. And go fuck yourself while you're at it. Axler's taught me more about how to improve myself than you ever will."

Jacob slid his arm out of Edwin's grip and stood back to watch Tommy place his ball on the tee. The edges of his vision widened as he relaxed his eyes and focused on Tommy. Edwin, Rose, the anger, the whole world disappeared. The sound of the metal struck his ears like a chime in an orchestra.

Jacob fixed his eyes on Tommy's form. His arms held the club high in the air as he watched the ball travel toward its intended target. Confidence bloomed from Jacob's chest into his cheeks; he was onto something. He walked to a different angle to watch the next drive. Again, Tommy held the ball between his thumb and middle finger, bent down to extend his right leg behind him, breathed out, and placed the tee. Jacob recorded everything. He watched the micro-movements of Tommy's hands, their position on the club; he noted where Tommy was breathing in his chest, how it dropped to his stomach just before he swung the club back. Another perfect hit. Another setup, another angle to watch.

"I'm ready. Let's play," said Jacob.

Who did Jacob think he was? thought Edwin. Jacob was mocking Tommy, the game of golf, his own father; he had no respect. Edwin removed his visor from his head and ran his hand through his thick hair. "Jacob, I told you—"

"Play? You think you're ready, huh? I have to see this," said Tommy.

Dennis, Thomas, Sr., and Edwin headed for the golf carts. Tommy and Jacob rode together.

The men asked Jacob to tee up. He imagined them scrutinizing his every move. He pictured sending the ball into the trees or missing it completely on the first stroke. But then from deep in his mind, he heard: *You are not Jacob. You are Thomas Murtaugh, Jr.* He projected a life-size hologram of Tommy, just as he'd seen him: elegant, cocksure, having fun, relaxed; then he stepped inside that image, walked over to the tee and set his ball down. He extended his right leg backward, breathed out, and took a swing. The white ball soared straight out until it dropped about two hundred yards in the middle of the fairway.

"Holy shit," Edwin yelled.

Dennis and the rest of the men clapped and patted Jacob on the back.

"That is an improvement," said Tommy. "But you're Irish, after all, me boy. We have to be sure it wasn't luck."

Jacob's game stayed constant. He kept watching Tommy, and his grandfather, and his Uncle Dennis, and his father, and he picked up more skills at every hole. The Murtaugh men noticed. Edwin smiled, cheered, patted Jacob on the back. Jacob resented his father's pride, for he had no right to it.

Jacob wanted to keep getting better at the game to win them over, and then dash it all, to destroy every hope they each could have that he might be a sportsman, a golfer, a Murtaugh after all.

Today Edwin would know the stench of rejection; he would taste the bitterness which seeps from the injury of daily neglect because it was he who had broken Jacob. He broke him by his absence, shattered him with his indifference, disabled him through his dissociation, and fractured him by not rescuing his son; he never saved him from the bullies, the scary adults, or from his crazy mother.

"I'm so proud of you, Son. Did you enjoy yourself today?" Edwin had no plans to apologize for being wrong. He'd already forgotten about the threat this morning. "Tommy said you've got real potential. He thinks you should join a golf camp. He could get you into—"

"Today wasn't about golf, Dad. I don't like golf. I hate

217

sports."

"You don't hate sports, Jacob. You just need more successes like you had today."

Jacob had set the trap; now Edwin was heading directly for it.

"You applied yourself out there, and it paid off. Your Papa is ecstatic. He wanted to dance a jig like he did the day you were born," Edwin smiled wildly.

"I wasn't applying myself to please Papa or anyone else. I was doing it to get better at Quantum Change. I wanted to prove it works. That I can do it better than anybody. Why can't you be proud of me for that?"

"Your Papa and your uncles don't understand Quantum Change. They understand golf."

"I'm not talking about them. I'm talking about you. You can't be proud of me unless I do something that matches your interests like golf, or clarinet, or marching band. Then you miss most of my games and concerts. Well, forget it. Impressing you isn't worth it anymore. I don't want to play sports, and I don't care if you can't be proud of me. I don't need it. I've found other people who are proud of me just the way I am."

"Like who, Rue? Raymond Axler? Have they put food on your table and clothes on your back? People like that aren't always going to be around, Jacob. But your family will be." Up came the finger to Jacob's face, shaking. "You've heard the saying, 'Blood is thicker than water,' and it's true. You go off with these people and treat them better than you treat us. You smile and act like a different person, but around us you're always fault-finding. They won't be there for you when the going gets tough."

"Fault-finding? You mean like you're doing now?" Jacob knew he needed to pull back. He wanted to stay in control. "You're right, Dad, I am two different people. That's because I'm changing. Our whole family has changed in the last couple of years. It's been painful for all of us. Things will be different when I go away to college."

"Go away? And just where do you plan to go? And who will pay for it?"

"I'm going to get scholarships and go somewhere far away." He hoped that hurt, but Edwin was likely more worried about college tuition than the cost of losing his son.

That evening, after the family dinner, Jacob and Melody were throwing clothes in their suitcases. Rose came to their suite. Her face was pulled tight. Her green eyes seemed to glow like a feral cat prowling for prey.

"Melody, go see your father. I need to talk to Jacob."

Melody raised her eyebrows and softly made tsk-tsk noises as she left the room.

"What's the matter, Mom?" asked Jacob.

"Did you and Paulo do something you shouldn't have?"

Jacob froze. "No, why?" He scanned his mother's face searching for what she really knew.

"Jacob, something happened. His mother spoke to me at dinner and said I should talk to you."

"Is Paulo okay?"

"Jacob, tell me the truth. You know it's always better if I find out the truth from you than if you lie to me."

"No, Mom, we were playing in the pool last night, I was throwing him around, we were having a good time.

Why?"

"She said she smelled alcohol on his breath. When she asked him about it he said you gave it to him, but you made him pull his pants down first."

"Oh that. He wanted to play truth or dare. It was in front of the others, and yeah, I gave him a sip. It was no big deal."

"No big deal? His mother is pissed, Jacob. And she's concerned. Giving your twelve-year-old cousin liquor and then making him get naked is inappropriate. What's wrong with you?"

"We were just playing around. I'm sorry."

"Sorry? After everything this family has been through? Everything we're still going through with your Grandaddy? I swear, Jacob, I just don't get you." She got up off the bed and left.

Jacob wondered if Paulo was upset with him. Should he go see him? Did his cousin think he was a freak? Paulo only told his mom about pulling his bathing suit off. He didn't mention anything else, or she would have complained about that, thought Jacob. He decided to leave him alone.

The next morning, before the Murtaughs left, Jacob stopped by Erik's room. His mother answered the door.

"I am sorry, but Erik went to the pier with a friend. He's missed you, Jacob. Too bad you are leaving. Here, let me write down our address so you can be penpals. Will you write him?"

"Yes, here's my address. Please tell him I said *es tut mir leid*."

"For what are you sorry, Jacob?"

"Just tell him for me. He'll understand." ❧

220

BOY IN THE HOLE

CHAPTER XVI

Candid Camera

Rich Valley (the locals called it Tampa's bedroom) was growing. Tampa Bay had become a choice venue for art and Broadway shows in Florida. There was a feverish push to connect it to Orlando with better interstates. Hotels and restaurants popped up between the cities faster than people earned money to book them.

Jacob began tenth grade at East Valley High School, a new school closer to the Murtaugh's home. He hoped being thrown into a larger school, hardly knowing anyone would prepare him for when he left the state to attend college. It was an opportunity to create a new version of himself. One of the changes he decided to make was to use his locker rather than haul his bookbag around. Memorizing the combination, sorting out what texts to carry for his upcoming classes, and arriving on time was daunting. The last time he tried using a locker was in ninth grade. He arrived five minutes late and was so anxious he developed a headache and berated himself for the rest of the day. So over the summer, he told his friend Miriam he was doing one of his psychology experiments and wished to pick her brain.

"So not carrying a book bag is going to get you a new image?" asked Miriam.

"Not having anxiety over using a locker is the start of a new image," said Jacob.

"Oh yeah. Hey everybody, look at that boy. He's not carrying a bookbag. I think I want to be his friend." Miriam snorted.

"Damn, when did you get so cynical?"

"I'm from the Bronx. I was born cynical."

"Well, Ms. Cynical from the Bronx, are you going to help me?"

"Go ahead," she laid her head on his lap (they were sitting on her couch) and propped her feet up on the armrest. "Analyze away, Dr. Freud."

"What's the first thing you do when you get to your locker in the morning?" Jacob carefully watched Miriam's eye movements. She tilted her head and looked up and to the right.

"I don't know, do you have to start with the hard questions, Jay?"

"Well, pretend you know, Mira. You get there and you're standing in front of that locker. What's going on?"

"I'm thinking about my day."

"Right, what do you see?"

"I'm just picturing my friggin' books in my arm walking to class. What do you want from me?" She waved her hands in the air like she was frantically guiding a plane into its parking spot.

"That's great. Here, have a Hershey's Kiss."

"You bastard. You know I'm tryin' to lose," she said, unwrapping the foil from the candy.

"There's more where that came from. And they can either be a reward or a punishment."

"How do you figure chocolate could ever be a punishment?"

"Since you want to lose weight, if you don't cooperate (he was speaking in his best German accent) vee vill force-fed them until you explode."

"You're so weird. This is why you need a new image."

"Right. So back to the locker. You said you picture your books in your arms. How do you know which ones to take with you?"

Miriam scrunched her face; several expressions swirled and twisted around like laundry on spin cycle. "I think about my schedule, when lunch is, where my classes are, so I know how many to carry, and when I can come back to my locker."

From her eye movements and gestures, Jacob discerned how Miriam planned her day. After a few more questions (and chocolate), he was able to recreate how she organized her thoughts so he could mentally install her strategy and use his locker without stress.

"You have such extraordinary certainty, Miriam. Even with something simple, like using a locker. I admire you."

"You're full of it, Jay. There's nothin' here to see."

"I disagree. I've not been able to trust myself to think ahead like you. I just wing it, bearing all that weight, literally and physically. I like your way better."

Everyone uses their brain, thought Jacob. They know how to speak when asked a question. They give their opinion, resolutely. But some brains shift and change shape like a sand dune in a storm. For where one stands affects what one sees. Most stand firmly, fixed in their perspective; whereas Jacob preferred to walk around a thing, get on top of it, look underneath it, see it this way and that way, never able to feel certain of the right way to look at it. Never able, that is until he watched others first and then could choose a mindset. People have knowledge they keep to themselves. But with Quantum Change, Jacob could unlock their secrets and hoard them like charms against ignorance and helplessness.

Another new behavior he'd learned was speed reading. He'd worked on the skill with Axler and was finishing homework assignments quicker than Rose thought best.

"You're not actually doing your homework, Jacob," she said, throwing his door open. "There's no way you're going to get good grades and get into college with these fantasies Raymond Axler is putting into your mind."

"What difference does it make if I finish my homework in thirty minutes or two hours?"

"Your grades are the difference. You're still making C's in math. You aren't studying enough."

"That's not true. I don't like math, so I spend less time on it. Besides, a C is passing."

"You've got to think of the SAT exam coming up and your GPA, Jacob. I'm not going to let you waste your future on Quantum Change."

"So, it's a waste of time now? Then what's the point in having Melody get treated by Rue? That's all Quantum

Change. And if it's such a waste of time, why do you ask for my help when you're depressed?"

Rose crossed her arms and stood over him. "You're changing, Jacob. I don't even recognize you. Where's my sweet little boy? You think you can act like Axler and get by in the world, but it's going to come crashing down on you. I'm not even sure you're sane."

"And what qualifications do you have to diagnose me?" Jacob overlooked the anger on Rose's hardened face and focused on the wild terror in her green eyes. *Should I push her fear? Eviscerate her soft underbelly and leave her bleeding?*

"You're like two different people. I think you're schizophrenic," said Rose. "And if you don't watch yourself I can have you put away."

"Okay, Mommie Dearest. You try that." He could cut her out of his life then and there, then she would have no one. *I'm all she has.* Jacob's inner voice faded, like an echo pitter-patters in a moist cave. *If you abandon her, she'll die*, said The Voice.

"You're grounded, Jacob. From now on you have to study every night for an hour and practice your clarinet for thirty minutes."

"Where do these arbitrary numbers come from?"

"It's what's recommended, Jacob."

"Recommended by whom, specifically?" challenged Jacob.

"I don't have to answer that. I've read, and I know."

"Okay, you win. But I'll be so busy studying, you'll never see me." Jacob couldn't dismember her from his life. But he'd learned a secret power from Axler: not to care, not to hold grudges, but to turn stone-cold indifferent.

AKIVA HERSH

With people outside his family, Jacob had mastered this flexibility. When someone upset him, he could act as if he could freeze time and ask, *If there were a thousand ways to respond, which is the most elegant? Which gets me what I want?* Then he could restart the flow of time and choose the best option. Not with Rose or Edwin. By living at home surrounded by their toxins, he became imbrued by his family's limitations, their faults, their model of the world. Like a parasite infests its host, his parents lived off the life he was trying to make for himself, siphoning nutrients, stealing the riches, and leaving the morsels.

Which is the reason Jacob's perversions festered. When Melody was asleep, and his parents watched Carson, Jacob snuck a towel from the bathroom and laid it across the gap under his door to hide the light. He had science to do. He took a thermometer out of his drawer, swabbed it with alcohol—the pungent smell gave him a hard-on, for by now the ritual had set in ungodly anticipation—and slowly inserted the silver tip into the hole of his penis. He laid against a pile of pillows naked and stroked, gently pushing in the thermometer halfway so he could feel the rigid glass through the surface of his frenulum. Determined, he pushed it all the way in, holding it so that it would not bob up and out. After a few minutes, he recorded the temperature in a journal and slurped the thermometer clean.

Next, he measured himself and wrote down the length and the girth and the width. Having worked himself into a frenzy, he pleasured himself until he orgasmed into a little plastic vial, measured the amount of semen and recorded it in the journal. He tasted the fresh batch and noted whether it was sweet, salty, or neutral, and wrote down what he had eaten in the last twenty-four hours. He had several vials stored. He shook them and noted their changing colors. This continued until the ritual no longer gave him a taboo vibe. He craved something edgier.

One day at the mall, he went to a bookstore and crept into the adult section. Finding a book on masturbation, he read the chapter about autofellatio. Using the techniques, he would ejaculate on his face instead of the in the vials. But this new ordinance wasn't enough for his appetite.

He snuck his father's Polaroid camera out of his closet and hid it in his room. Late at night, between the measuring and the autofellatio, he photographed his penis from various angles and lighting. He then cut out shapes and arranged them on his desk and jerked off to them. *How to dispose of these? Can't. They could be found. And they're too good to get rid of. Where to hide them?* He put them in a little blue safe Audrey had given him on his eighth birthday. It didn't lock securely; a spin on the combination dial latched it and gave the illusion of a lock.

This self-made porn helped him get off for weeks until he moved on to other fetishes.

Jacob laid the reed on the mouthpiece of his clarinet. Jazz band was the last period of the day. Mr. Hove, the band director, handed Jacob a goldenrod hall pass and said, "They want you in the front office. Your father is waiting."

Had someone died? What was the emergency?

The entire trip home, Edwin shifted the conversation,

bit his nails, turned on the radio, flipped channels, and explained nothing more than, "Your mother is upset and wants to talk to you."

Jacob followed Edwin into his parents' room. On the bed sat his little blue safe. Rose was next to it, eyes red from crying; mascara mottled down her lashes over her eyes.

"These are disgusting, Jacob."

"What are you doing going through my drawers?" Jacob asked, scrambling to invent a story.

"I was cleaning," said Rose.

"In my sock drawer?"

She had been rummaging, as she had done for years.

"I was putting away socks, and I wiped the lid of that safe; it flipped open, and all these dicks popped out. Are they yours?"

"Yes," he said.

"Have you taken any pictures of your sister? Have you touched her?"

"No, Mom. This has nothing to do with her."

"Enough, Rose leave him alone," said Edwin. "Boys go through phases like this—"

"Why are you defending this perversion, Edwin? Never mind, of course you are. Jacob, you're grounded. Go to your room and stay out of my sight." Rose leaped from the bed and pointed to the door as if Jacob had any doubts about where his room was.

Jacob stopped photographing himself. But his parents didn't tell him to return the Polaroid camera. Before it was confiscated, he hoped to pull off one more plan.

One of his friends from church, Riley (a year younger than Jacob), invited him to spend the night one Saturday, and they would go to church together the next day. Riley was the son of an Air Force pilot. He was built like a baseball player, and every muscle in his body was toned. He worked out and liked to show off his six-pack. Jacob hoped to persuade him to let him take some pictures.

Riley stepped out of the shower and came into his bedroom wrapped in a white, cotton towel tied right below his bellybutton. His short skater hair dripped. His towel split just past his knees all the way to his ankles, revealing his brawny calves.

"Whadya think?"

Jacob couldn't say what he thought, imagining those legs wrapped around his face. "It's kinda dark in here," said Jacob pointing the camera at Riley.

"We can't go anywhere else. My parents might wake up."

"Let's just turn all the lights on."

Riley posed in the towel, and Jacob snapped some shots of his abs, pecs, and biceps. The camera buzzed and whirred and spat out pictures on white squares that looked washed out and creepy, but Jacob's memories of Riley's form were imprinted on his brain forever.

Riley let Jacob pull the towel aside to show more leg.

"Your skin is a lot whiter up there than on your chest."

"Yeah, but at least I'm growin' some hair. I've got some pubes, do you?"

"Yeah, a little brown nest," said Jacob.

"Look," said Riley. He pulled the towel down and displayed a few, light brown whips.

"Do you count them? I bet you count them. What

about under your arms?"

Riley lifted his arms, and Jacob posed it in the air as though he were sculpting a statue. "Stay just like that." Jacob snapped a few more shots. "Nice," said Jacob cautiously.

"I have an idea. What if I took some pics of your dick, and we put it in a girl's mailbox as a prank?"

"That's hilarious. Okay."

"So, drop the towel."

Riley felt himself. "We should watch TV for a little while. Make sure the parents are asleep."

They sat in his bed, side by side, each going through various phases of arousal. After a tentative start to another photoshoot, Riley said, "I don't think it's gonna work tonight. I'm tired."

Jacob played it cool.

The next morning, when Jacob was brushing his teeth, Riley asked if he could come in the bathroom.

"I need to pee."

"Yeah, fine," Jacob said dryly.

The position of Riley's mirror was such that while Jacob was brushing, he could see Riley's reflection. Riley took his time unzipping, let his pants fall to the floor, then his underwear, and held a very large penis in his hand. He pulled on it a couple of times then urinated, looking at Jacob in the eyes. Jacob wanted to say many things, but he kept his mouth shut and memorized the scene. He brushed his teeth, moving the toothbrush in and out, very slowly. Maybe Riley only objected to having his picture taken. ❧

BOY IN THE HOLE

CHAPTER XVII

God is Nowhere

During the summer between tenth and eleventh grade, Jacob worked as a camp counselor at Messiah Lutheran. He resented Rose and Edwin pushing him to get a summer job. He was ready for free time, but they wanted him to have cash to spend and to "develop a work ethic."

Jacob enjoyed being around the children and teaching classes; the part-time position also gave him time to study Quantum Change, purchase more psychology books, and apprentice with Rue in the evenings.

Jacob was a popular counselor. When recess was over, he would stand on the sandy hill by the edge of the large parking lot turned playground and yell, "Let's go!" With a quick pivot walked toward the classrooms. Basketballs dropped, children running between bases changed directions, boys and girls let go of monkey bars; fifty kids ran after him. That method didn't work for anyone else.

Jacob always gave the morning devotional. He told

the children a modern fable with (he was crafty at making up stories) which contained some moral or lesson he wanted to impart about building good character, encouragement, or caution. Then he told a Bible story that undergirded the fable and sent the kids on their way.

He taught one Bible class and one elective to boys and girls eight and up. He persuaded the church to purchase a camcorder for the elective. The campers could vote whether to act out a morning news show and weather report, shoot a summer camp horror flick or interview each other in a mock talk show.

Every day, a blue-eyed boy with sandy brown hair made a point to sit on the front row of Jacob's classes. He followed Jacob everywhere and declared himself Teacher's Assistant. The boy turned gloomy when he had to go to another class and couldn't be with Jacob. Marcy, the camp director, spoke to his grandmother one day when she picked him up.

"Nathan talks about Jacob all the time," said Mrs. Vinker. "The attachment is no surprise to us. His mother has been divorced for a while, and his father isn't in the picture. There's no steady man who pays him any attention. Jacob is good for him."

Marcy and the other counselors agreed to let Nathan stay with Jacob all day.

"Can I eat with you?" asked Nathan. He set his brown bag on Jacob's desk and scooted up a chair.

"Of course you can. How do you get so tan living in Maryland all year long?" asked Jacob.

"It's from my mom. She tells me I have olive skin and sparkly eyes. See?" He moved his head close to Jacob's face and pulled his eyelid down with his finger. "She says if you look real close, you can see gold flecks in my blue eyes. Can you?"

"She's right. You have beautiful blue eyes," said Jacob. "How old are you, Nathan?"

"Thirteen. I'll be fourteen in December. My mother is deaf, you know. You make thirteen like this in ASL." He took Jacob's hand and shaped it like a thumbs up. "Now put up two fingers and wave them, like you're saying, 'Come here.'"

"I'll have to remember that," said Jacob.

"My grandma says I can invite you over to our house to play. Wanna come?" Nathan bounced his knee up and down. Jacob watched the lines and curves of the muscles working his tan, hairless leg.

"Yeah, I'd like to. How would you like to go see a movie first?"

"That would be rad. What do you want to see?"

"Who Framed Roger Rabbit?"

"Yes! My grandparents don't want to see it. I was afraid I'd miss it."

Nathan had to eat with Jacob every day. It wasn't long before Jacob began giving Nathan a ride home from camp and picking him up in the morning. If Jacob was sitting down, Nathan was beside him. Is this how a father feels about his son? Jacob wondered. But a father wouldn't stare when Nathan's skin glistened with water, dripping from his shoulders and chest as he climbed out of the pool and sat on the edge to dry in the wind.

He's so beautiful.

Would a father look forward to the way Nathan ran

to his car in the morning, his hair wet, his skin smelling like soap (Nathan always wanted a hug)?

The way he tosses his hair; his soft hands; his full ruby lips.
The caged beast beats its chest. It beats and beats.
Jacob was overcome by strange feelings. Something wanted to break out. The guard is about to turn the key; the match head is scraping across the gritty sand about to flash brilliantly; the cloud is ready to burst.

You are disgusting, said The Voice. *You're just like Klaus.*

Changing in the locker room at the pool, Jacob saw Nathan in his underwear. He didn't want to see more. Didn't want to touch. Or, maybe he didn't want to desire to see more. But he liked to look at the shape of Nathan's fingers, he liked to stroke the blonde hairs on his neck, he liked to have the boy's hand in his; he loved to listen to Nathan talk and talk and talk.

The Vinkers invited Jacob to their beach house for the weekend. Jacob and Nathan sailed, fished, grilled, walked the beach, and slept in the same bed. Mrs. Vinker took several photos of the two of them and gave them to Jacob in an album.

"Why didn't you have your own room?" Rose questioned.

"Nathan told me there was a double bed and said we'd be sleeping in it. It was innocent, Mom."

"You're the adult. That old couple doesn't know any better, Jacob. You need to be careful around all these boys."

"He's three years younger than me. And I'm not an

adult. I'm sixteen."

She was stacking her dismay; now it's a boy named Nathan, then there was Paulo. There had been others. And she was right to worry, but she wouldn't say more. Her growing list of objections and vague accusations adumbrated what she feared Jacob was like a police sketch artist makes a composite drawing from multiple descriptions—none in isolation are accurate—but when put together, a recognizable face emerges. A face she did not want to see.

One morning, during the last week of camp, there was a pink envelope on Jacob's desk. On the back, Nathan had drawn a heart with an arrow through it. A card with a puppy on the front held a picture of Nathan wearing only shorts, smiling, looking coy. The card said:

I'm going to miss you. Here is my address and my phone number. I love you so much.

Nathan

Every night of the last week, Jacob stayed with Nathan at the Vinkers until bedtime. He tucked him in and waited until he fell asleep and left. Was something wrong with him? Should he tell someone? Who? This was what people gossiped about on talk shows. He was a freak. You got put in jail for this and men beat you up and raped you. *You're a baby-fucker like Klaus*, screamed The Voice. Was he like Klaus? What made him this way?

Flashes of fragmented images darted across the screen of his mind like sparks. A finger, hands, water, a toothy smile, nothing he could make sense of. Was he broken? Did something happen to him to make him a monster?

When Nathan left Rich Valley at the end of the summer, Jacob promised he'd write. They exchanged pictures and called each other occasionally.

"Did you get my last card? Did you see my mom?" asked Nathan.

"I did. She's very pretty. I can see where you get your good looks from."

"Who knows, maybe you'll want to marry her," Nathan said. "You can come up here for Christmas and meet her."

"I'll be spending Christmas with my family. We'll have to wait to see each other this summer. But I am mailing you a Christmas present I think you'll like."

"Cool, what is it?"

"No way. You have to wait until it gets to you."

Jacob bought him some action figures he liked to collect, wrapped them, and sent them in time to be put under his tree.

Jacob feared Heaven would never accept him. There was not a storm powerful enough to cleanse the filth staining his soul. His desolation cast him into depression. Rose called Pastor Rogers to come speak with him.

"Jacob, nothing can separate us from the love of God," said Pastor Rogers.

"I don't mean to argue, Pastor. But sin separates us."

"Is there something you've done that you feel is keeping you from God?"

"Everyone sins," said Jacob.

"And everyone can be forgiven if they confess their sins. Is there something you're holding back?"

"Of course not. The Bible says no one can hide from God." Jacob had little reason to believe Pastor Rogers had any solution to his ordeal. He figured his only hope was to keep the conversation on a theological level. "I don't feel God. He's nowhere."

"Jacob, would you get me a piece of paper and a pencil?" Jacob brought him a notebook and pen from the kitchen drawer. "Please come sit beside me. It may surprise you to know that even clergy can feel that God is distant. But look at this." On the paper, Pastor Rogers wrote: God is nowhere. "What do you see?"

"God is nowhere," said Jacob.

"Right. And sometimes life looks that way," said Rogers. "And the Devil wants you to think that. But watch this." He drew a line dividing now and here. "Tell me what you see."

"God is now here," read Jacob.

"Sometimes the way we look at a situation affects the way we experience it. God is here all the time. We just have to give Him the space to show us."

Pastor Rogers was a nice man and was beloved among the faithful at Messiah Lutheran. Jacob could see why. He laid in his bed that night thinking over what Pastor Rogers wrote on the paper. It was a nice trick. ❧

CHAPTER XVIII

His Loss, Her Gain

"How could you have lost your job, Edwin? They don't just fire a General Manager over a misunderstanding," said Rose, dumping a bag of rice into the boiling water. She knew the kids resented being served her chicken and yellow rice every week, but there were no Lean Cuisine meals to microwave, and she was in no mood to prepare a real meal.

"Of course they don't, but I'm telling you, every day for the last year I've had five people looking over my shoulder waiting for me to make a mistake. They're all gunning for my job. I think one of them framed me."

Of course, Rose thought, if he hadn't cheated in the company Christmas raffle by stuffing extra entries from family members, the ne'er-do-wells might not have become suspicious when his daughter and his mother-in-law won first and third prize. And it didn't help he ratted on himself to his buddy Jim, the set-designer.

They had their little secrets, like schoolgirls in a club. Rose was suspicious of the two of them, the way they carried on and seemed to fall all over each other in the store whenever one of them had an idea for a new fabric layout or room design. Maybe they had a spat, and Jim told on him.

"It doesn't matter, Edwin. What are we going to do?"

"I'll look for something. Don't worry."

One morning, Edwin came out of the bathroom to find Rose already out of bed.

"You're getting up early," he said.

"I have a job interview today." She stepped into the closet and slid a bright yellow dress across the rack.

"A job interview? Where?"

She put her finger on a gray and white dress. "The Presbyterian church on Peters Avenue." She took the dress off the hanger and laid it on the bed, then went searching for matching heels. A church secretary needed to look sharp but conservative, she thought. She wanted to be memorable, not garish.

Edwin watched her. She looked like a child playing dress-up. Except for the furniture store they owned in Pierceville, she had never been in the workforce. Her anxiety kept her awake most nights. How would she wake up every morning, get on all that makeup, dress, eat, and show up to do a job?

"Who's going to take care of the kids?" Edwin asked her.

"Jacob can take care of himself," said Rose. "He works after school anyway. He drives. If we need him to run Melody somewhere, he can. She'll ride the bus home and let herself in. It's a part-time job. I'll be home soon after her."

What bothered Edwin wasn't Rose working to supplement their income. Getting out of the house and into a regular schedule might be good for her. The trouble with Rose working was the necessity of it; any ache or agony as a result of having to help the family would be another tear for her to collect and display in her lacrimatory—of which she had filled several—and they were all testimonies to his failure as a husband and provider.

"Why don't you hold off, Rose? The job at Rooms To Go is only temporary. I'll keep looking for something better."

"I can't hold off. Your salary is half what you were making at Masi. It's been months, and you haven't landed a single job interview. How many thousands of dollars have you borrowed from Tommy? Forget waiting. I'm going to get a job."

And she did. She was hired as the secretary at Valley Presbyterian Church where she met Bruce. He looked like he had peeled himself off a vintage package of Brawny paper towels when he strolled into the pastor's office. He was tall. His bright blue, checkered flannel shirt matched his eyes. He had shoulder-length, sandy blonde hair and an unruly beard and mustache.

"Well, hello there. What'd they do with the old woman?"

"Mrs. Flemming? She retired." Rose put out her hand, which drooped and wilted in the air like a full-white lily. "I'm the new secretary. I'm Rose."

He looked at it and smiled at the quaint gesture. He thought about kissing it, but decided to see where she would take him first.

"Yes, you are, and what an improvement. I'm Bruce," He shook her hand with a firm grip. "Is Pastor Carlton here?"

"Not yet. Do you have an appointment?"

"Sort of. I stop by every Tuesday."

"Every Tuesday?"

"Me and the wife are on the rocks. Guess that means I'll be seeing more of you."

"Because of the trouble?" Rose was flustered.

"Because I come here every week to talk about it," Bruce said. "When I'm done it'll be about lunchtime. Won't you be hungry?"

"I bring my lunch. What do you do?"

"Whatever I can to piss that bitch off. How about we go grab some food after I talk to the good pastor?"

Rose pitied him. She had learned something from Rue; perhaps she could be a friend to Bruce. She caught her eyes looking at his crotch. Just then, he leaned back in his chair, spreading his legs wider. She cleared her throat and looked through the drawers of her desk, pretending to search for something.

"Yes, lunch will be fine," she said.

"Fine? Do you want to or don't you?"

"Yes, I want to."

So disjunction set into the Murtaugh family, like a disease, and secrecy, and the two pressed the form of the family itself into a new thing, like a mask transforms the face of the wearer; like an actor on stage, voice booming, reciting lines from a script he did not write, feeling himself a fake, drawn by the golden spotlight cast on the stage floor like a trap; the family was alone, except for disjunction and secrecy, each vigilant to drown out any voice that would break the spell.

Driving down a long stretch of road from work one rainy evening, three things converged upon Edwin which overpowered his perceptions and threw him into a reality over which he had no control.

Sitin' On The Dock of the Bay played on the radio; Edwin sang along with Otis Redding. Far behind Edwin's car, red lights flashed, and he heard a siren. At that moment, a helicopter flew overhead. The rain slashing his windshield and the whipping palm trees lining the road morphed into the jungle of Vietnam. Edwin's heart thrashed his rib cage.

I have to help that helicopter. It's going to get shot down, God Dammit.

He pulled the car to the roadside. He had better radio for help, but communications were jammed. He opened his door and was nearly sideswiped by a motorcycle. Edwin ran around the back of his car and dropped to the ground to avoid the barrage of bullets. Raindrops beat against his head. His shirt, tie, and pants were soaked and muddy.

Is that blood? God, am I hit?

He crawled on his knees and elbows into the ditch to wait for the chopper to land. The siren screamed past him. A car pulled up behind Edwin.

The driver walked over. "Sir, are you okay?"

"Get down," Edwin shouted at the man.

"Is there somebody I can call for you?" He walked

closer to Edwin and put his hand on his shoulder. "Hey, let me help you. It's gonna be all right."

When Rue arrived at the Murtaughs, Melody let her in. "Daddy is in the bedroom with Jacob and Mommy."

"All right, love, and how are you?"

"I'm scared."

"I bet you are. Let's go check on him." She took Melody by the hand. Edwin had curled himself into a fetal position on the floor. Jacob rubbed his back. Rose sat with her head in her hands.

"Let me speak with Edwin, people. But stay close."

They all waited on the living room couch. Over the next hour, wails and screams announced something was still happening; they heard Rue's stern but reassuring voice over Edwin's whimpers. She was walking him through memories of Vietnam; she was in the trench, next to him in battle, watching his buddies get slaughtered.

Rue didn't run away from scary shit, thought Jacob. He wanted to be like her, not like his father, who survived a horrible war only to run and hide from the horrors of daily life, like being a husband and father. He was a coward.

"Jacob, your father needs you," called Rue. Jacob felt his stomach sink. He didn't want to go, didn't want to have to be stronger than Edwin or to have to help him through whatever it was he was hiding from. But his teacher had called him, and he couldn't refuse her.

When he walked in, the two of them looked like a living reenactment of Michelangelo's Pietà; Edwin was sprawled out on the floor and his head laid against Rue's bosom. They looked up at Jacob. Edwin was sweaty and exhausted; Rue was stressed and in need of a cigarette.

"I'm so sorry, son. So, so sorry," Edwin whimpered.

A part of Jacob wanted to ask what he was sorry for; he wanted to help the confession along, but another part wanted Edwin to figure out whatever this was on his own.

All of life is warfare, thought Jacob. Every day is a step closer to death. Having seen his father so needy, Jacob extended him mercy since Edwin could not comprehend that the only life one lives is exactly the moment one experiences. Life flees from one's grip every instant. Death, then, is the result of one leaving behind a single moment in time—not the loss of past, present, or future. No, Edwin was tethered to the past; he was therefore not living, could never live, for everything that he could lose, he already had.

"It's going to be okay, Dad." Jacob forced himself to look at his father.

He might kill himself, said The Voice.

Click and nod. It will be okay.

"What's happening with your father is a condition called Post-Traumatic Stress Disorder. We knew the soldiers coming home were stuffing what they saw and heard, and that it had to come out later on. This is it, Jacob."

Edwin asked if he could go to the bathroom. Rue indicated she wanted to step outside.

"So how is it treated, Rue?"

"Quantum Change shows promise. The research is

still out because we're just now seeing men like your father come in with such severe symptoms. Losing his job, the stress on the marriage, the molestation, all of it is a pressure cooker, and he's cracking."

"He needs to see you more often," said Jacob.

"I agree. But he's passive-aggressive as hell, you know that. He may well use this so that he gets to be sicker than Melody and Rose."

"You mean everyone else has been in the spotlight, so he's going to steal it for a while?"

"Exactly," said Rue, curling her lip in disgust.

"With Dad jobless and going crazy, I may never get out of Rich Valley. I'm so fucking tired of all this, Rue."

"I know, love. I know."

"Jacob, a letter came from Blake," Rose called from the kitchen. Jacob ran from his room. They hadn't spoken on the phone in months. Blake had been busy with his senior year, Jacob, with his family.

Jacob opened the letter and saw his name cased in large type at the top. Underneath, Blake had typed between two icons of a quill and scroll:

I THOUGHT I WOULD TRY A NEW PROGRAM CALLED "THE PRINT SHOP" FOR THE LETTERHEAD. HOPE YOU LIKE IT!
(Now by hand)
When are you coming up again? Do you have a disk drive on your computer? If you do, will it use

normal floppy disks? Hope so! I got some games to give you. What did you get for Christmas? Me? I got a used car. Remember that Buick Skylark my grandparents were driving? They gave it to me! And I got this computer. How's your Bonsai? Did those trees live that we got? Get your behind up here soon!
(Then in type between two icons of computers)
HOPE TO SEE YOU SOON!
YOUR FRIEND, BLAKE WOLF
SAY HI TO YOUR PARENTS AND SISTER FOR ME.

Jacob wrote him back right away. How did you talk about your life with someone who knew your family but didn't know the ugliest parts you had to deal with from the moment you opened your eyes in the morning to when you tried to shut the world out at night?

He wrote about visiting colleges with his mother in Austin, Ann Arbor, and their upcoming visit scheduled to Irvine, California. Jacob decided a private Lutheran college was the best option if he could keep up the grades, get the scholarships, and persuade Uncle Tommy to foot the rest of the tuition. Otherwise, he'd be stuck at home, in hell, going to the local community college. He hoped that didn't offend Blake if he was considering the community college; it was the prospect of living with his family that would be hell.

He mentioned his parents bought him a used car, too. It was a turquoise 1963 Mercury Meteor with green leather seats and whitewall tires. It had three horns that motorists in the next town could hear.

He was looking forward to the new Batman movie coming out. In preparation, Jacob affixed a large Batman sticker to the windshield of his car. His friends at school were already calling it the Batmobile.

No, the saplings died, but the Bonsai was living. It was a lot of work to keep up. He suspected Melody wouldn't take care of it while he was away for college.

Hopefully, the next time they spoke, Jacob would know his major for sure, but he thought it might be psychology. He hoped Blake would call soon. He planned to see him in the middle of the summer.

What Jacob couldn't write was that his family had fallen apart. No one spent time with each other; his parents never told each other, "I love you." Everybody was in therapy. His Baptist grandfather was a pervert. And just when he was supposed to be figuring out who he was and what he wanted out of life, he had to protect his sister, watch out for his father, and keep his eye on his mother because something strange was going on with her.

Love, Jacob.

Edwin was closing the store; he would be home late. Melody was at a sleepover. Rose walked out of the bedroom in black heels, a new black and white, low-cut dress, her lips splashed with cardinal-red, high-gloss lipstick. Her perfume grabbed Jacob's nose across the house.

"Where are you going?" asked Jacob.

"I thought you were going to a movie," Rose said, startled.

"I am. Later. So where are you going?"

"Out with a girlfriend," she said.

"Who?"

"Who? A girlfriend from church."

"You don't have any girlfriends from church. You're mad at everyone there, Mom."

"Not our church. From Valley Presbyterian."

"Mom, you know Quantum Change has trained me to notice micro-behavior. You're anxious. Your breathing rate has increased. Your face is flushed. You're showing signs of distress which usually accompany behaviors of deception. What's going on?"

"I'm going on a date, Jacob. Please don't tell your father, will you?"

"I won't. It's with Bruce, isn't it?"

"Yes, and we care about each other deeply. He's everything your father isn't. I'll tell you all about it later, okay?"

That was more than Jacob had asked for; he just wanted the truth. But Rose wanted to confide in him, wanted a friend to reassure her she had done nothing wrong. Jacob could help her find the things to say and do to steer Bruce into leaving his wife. He'd been dragging his feet on account of the kids. Maybe Jacob could even counsel him, she thought. All he needed was to give Bruce a little push. He'd make his move, then she would leave Edwin, and they could start their new life together. She'd finally be free of it all, the poverty, the sadness.

"I'll be home before your father. We're just going to dinner. We'll talk then, okay, hon?"

"I'll be at that movie with my friends."

"Can't you miss it? Now that you know, I want to go over it all with you. I think you can help."

"There's a bunch of us going, Mom. I'm driving everyone. Maybe later this weekend."

"Fine, but I'm your mother. I should come first. But have fun and don't tell your sister either. I love you."

He watched her fluff her hair and grab the keys. He didn't know whom to feel sorrier for, Edwin, Melody, himself, or Rose; he knew Bruce was using her to relieve the stress from his marriage. As soon as the pressure was gone, Bruce would drop her, no matter what condition Rose was in when the time came. There was no way her dream to escape her present misery was going to happen by running off with him. It didn't work with Edwin; it wouldn't happen with Bruce. No man would save her from herself. ❧

CHAPTER XIX

On This Rock

Jacob played clarinet in a band at Messiah Lutheran. Some weekends they went on tour and played concerts at churches around Florida. After a long drive to a church outside of Miami one Friday night, the band unloaded the sound equipment into the sanctuary. The concert would be the next day with a carnival to follow, and a youth baseball game that evening.

Jacob's housemate for the trip was one of his best friends, Connor, the band leader's son. He was a freshman at the community college. He was tall and slender with shoulder-length hair, the hair of a drummer in a metal band. He made Jacob laugh harder than anyone else.

Jacob wanted to spend every free moment with Connor, much to Rose's dismay, because Connor reminded her of Wayne; he had the "gay humor," she said, complaining to Edwin. She didn't like the way he let his wrists go limp or how he flashed his blue eyes and toothy smile at Jacob. She knew he was queer, and Jacob did not need an older gay teen's influence when he only had a year of school left and would soon be beyond her control.

"You have no clue if Connor is gay," said Edwin.

"I do too know. I have an instinct."

"You have a son who is making friends. Weren't you complaining last year he only had female friends?"

"This boy is different," she said. "Why did Jacob have to choose an effeminate friend?"

Edwin flicked his wrist in mockery. "Effeminate like Wayne was?"

"I hope you live to regret saying that, Edwin Murtaugh."

Jacob and Connor ate dinner with their host family, an elderly couple. The boys entertained them with stories of antics from the band trips, performed impressions of Ronald Regan, and were tolerant with the host father when he wanted to discuss the Bible.

Shortly after ten o'clock, the hosts were ready for bed. They turned off the television, all the lights, and locked the doors, never giving a thought the evening might still be young for college and high school-aged boys.

Jacob and Connor lay side by side on the floor instead of on the beds their hosts had prepared. They told jokes and tried to muffle their giggles, each putting a hand over the other's mouth. Connor's over-jocular perspective could flip flop a somber occasion into a merry-go-round scene of vaudeville and hoopla. And why not? How would you cope with being tagged and collared; your soul marked as an abomination? You would make the best of the situation and find pleasure wherever you could.

Jacob knew they were simpatico because of their common condition; they were like prisoners outcast on a remote island, each thinking he was alone, until one day a faint pillar of black smoke pierces the line of trees in the distance. Is it a savage or another fugitive? The only thing to do is build a fire, too.

After days of waiting, the thin line of smoke tapers and vanishes against the blue sky. What has happened? The prisoner treks through the unspoiled forest, making his own path toward the faded signal.

A rustling just ahead cripples his resolve, but before he can turn and run, a merry face greets him in the clearing.

Each is no longer alone; they had been untouchables, but now compatriots.

"How long are you going to live at home, Connor? Aren't you sick of it?"

"My parents are cool. They let me come and go, mostly."

"Your parents are cool, that's true. But still, if I were you, I'd feel like I was in prison." Jacob rolled over on his side to face Connor. He had his shirt off. Jacob wanted to run his finger along the deep crevice between his pecs. "It's not like you can bring a date home or anything," Jacob said, investigating Connor's eyes, watching his chest rise and fall, scanning for any tension which might betray disagreement.

"Who would I bring home? I'm not dating anybody."

"You're not interested in some girl? Come on, a handsome guy like you shouldn't be single." Jacob hoped his words would catch in Connor's mind, like a chain on a bike switching cogs.

"Are you saying you think I'm cute?" Connor propped himself up on his elbow.

"Well, yeah. I bet all the girls chase you." Jacob wanted to backpedal.

"Not interested," said Connor. He gave Jacob an impish smile and watched, unmoving, like a tiny plastic Christmas elf propped up on a tree limb.

"Me either," said Jacob. Should he lean in to kiss him? Connor had parted his lips. He leaned forward a half an inch. Jacob moved his eyes from Connor's face to his chest, back to his open mouth. Jacob bit his bottom lip (Axler had taught him this was a universal sign of flirtation). Connor's breathing was undisturbed and cadenced, but he was the drummer of the band. Maybe he had more control over his body than most.

Jacob pressed his lips to Connor's and breathed him in. Connor pushed his tongue into Jacob's mouth. Jacob fell back onto his pillow, and Connor rolled on top of him.

Jacob pushed Connor away suddenly.

"Why the hell haven't you said anything before now?"

"Me? I've been trying to tell you for months."

"When?" Jacob asked.

"That day in the sanctuary when you were working on your new song for the band."

They had talked about the best key in which to write the song. Connor said the feeling of the rhythm dictates the key. Jacob countered it was the meaning of the words. They debated back and forth, neither realizing they weren't speaking of keys at all. For both were discovering the other's inner world, the hidden passages leading to desire and longing. Connor liked the major keys. Jacob liked the black notes; they brought out a deeper emotion, he thought. They agreed on both; Jacob wrote in a key change—then they stared at each other, neither needing to say a word. The silence between them became the music.

It was the intensity of the register that made Jacob look away. When he returned to Connor's face, his expression hadn't changed, as if to say, *I see you. I see who you are and what you're about*—which made Jacob look away again, pretending to study the notes on the staff paper. What made him look away wasn't a reluctance to go further but the opportunity, the chance that Connor was like him.

"I knew there was more going on. I tried to tell you the best way I could," said Connor.

"I thought you were into Heather. There were rumors she gave you a blowjob on the last band trip when she snuck into your tent, so I thought—"

"I did her a favor and took her to prom, nothing more. It was you I wanted to have in my sleeping bag. When nothing else happened, I kept my distance, at least in that way."

The next morning, the band played for the church. Jacob couldn't look at Connor; every drum beat and cymbal crash was like a question: *Are you thinking about last night? When can we do that again? What happens now?*

Jacob looked up at the stained-glass window. The church called it the "Passion Window" because it depicted symbols from the Lord's Supper. A large cluster of purple grapes hung above Jesus' shoulder. On the other side were golden stalks of wheat. By his right foot was a red and yellow rooster, to his left were three black nails, and hanging over his head grew a gnarly, thorny bush; three enormous drops of blood were falling from the thorns. Christ was standing with his arms held out wide, in crucifixion pose, or was it an embrace?

What struck Jacob, as he played his solo during *Spirit In The Sky*, were the symbols, the icons of death and betrayal, surrounding Jesus all the time. If Jacob's own life were a stained-glass window, he would be on a tiny, brown sinking ship in the middle of a blue and green ocean, naked, hands outstretched to Connor, also naked, walking toward him on the water. Jesus is on the other side of the boat in his white gown, bearing his cross, begging for Jacob's attention. Above Jacob is Rue, appearing like the Holy Mother with her golden light shining on him. Hovering above Jacob's shoulder is his mother cast as a devil, pitchfork about to strike. Over his other shoulder, his father hangs from a rope on a scraggly branch, like Judas. Melody's white ghostly body is floating dead in the water.

After the concert, Jacob tried to be busy. To avoid Connor, he helped set up booths and served food. In his mind he prayed over and over, like a mantra, like an obsession, *Lord, I don't know what you want from me, but if you don't show me your will and let me know what you want for my life, something is going to break in me.*

On the softball field later that evening, a boombox blasted Christian music. Jacob stood in the outfield.

Show me a sign, Lord. I can't take this. Connor was on the other team. He struck out. The teams switched, and it was Jacob's turn to bat. He smacked the ball past an outfielder and made it to second base. He stood there in the bright ballpark lights waiting for the next batter. Cut grass and cotton candy scents mated, creating a sweet earthy smell that seemed to run the bases. *We Exalt Thee* by Petra came on. Jacob sang along softly. The batter swung and missed. *Strike two.* Jacob focused on the lyrics. The metallic sound of the bat and the cheers of the crowd had been drowned out by the music. *Foul!* Tears fell from Jacob's eyes as the chords moved through him. The ball rolled on the ground past the pitcher. "Run, Jacob." He felt his body traveling to third base. He heard a voice from behind his head: *I love you, Jacob and I am going to use you. I am calling you, Jacob, for my purposes. Look at all of these people. You will lead my flock. Come home to me.* PING! The next batter hit the ball out of the park. "Run home, Jacob. Get home!"

As far as Jacob was concerned, he had had a religious experience on the baseball field. According to the pastor at Messiah Lutheran, to become a pastor, one had to be called by a church to go into the ministry. But Jacob knew the stories of Martin Luther, Paul, and other church fathers. They received a higher calling, and he had promised if it ever happened to him, he would obey.

He made the announcement to the band on the trip home the next day. Almost everyone said they were waiting for Jacob to catch up. They felt it was inevitable he was going to be a pastor. Everyone except Connor.

"Yeah, they get to try out all the best fashions," jabbed

Connor from the back seat. His mother glared at him.

"Just kidding, Jay. I'm happy for you."

The joke stung. He wanted Connor to be civil. He tried to speak to him alone at a gas stop.

"Don't sweat it, Pastor Murtaugh, all is well."

"Connor, stop it. It's beyond my choice. God has called me. You don't know what that's like."

"I know bullshit when I smell it. I think you're scared," he said.

"I told you what happened, Connor. It was like something right out of the Bible. I'm sorry you don't believe me. This isn't my choice anymore."

Like Jesus founded his church on Peter's faith, Jacob had discovered his own rock on which to build his future. He couldn't deny his feelings; he loved God and he loved boys, but what he could do was remove his ability to choose between them.

God revealed a plan to use Jacob to make his life meaningful. Whenever the doubts or regrets came, Jacob had a time and a place, a landmark he could point back to and declare: Here is the altar I built, and God was there; this is the place I sacrificed myself and the future I could have had, and God accepted it as good. On this spot, I was resurrected and was formed into a new thing. ❧

CHAPTER XX

The Fabric of Reality

Jacob came home from school to a cold, darkened house, silent as fog. He peered into his parents' room. A candle flame flickered on Rose's nightstand. He could see her body swaddled in sheets and comforters. Her silhouette was etched on the wall like hieroglyphics in an Egyptian tomb. She was weeping.

Finding her lying in state meant she had not been to work but had been in bed all day hiding from the world that wounded her. A cross look from a stranger or an ambiguous tone in a friend's voice sent her to the crypt where priests (her candles and music) covered her with natron and wrapped her bodily shell in strips of linen victimhood. Amulets of grudges and jealousy were carefully wrapped over her heart to protect her against further assaults along her journey.

Had anyone else suffered such inflictions, they would have gone about their day nursing their pride or feeling emotionally raw. Some might reach for comfort food, or a drink, or two or three. But not Rose. When life didn't measure up to her expectations, the failure brought on a near-death experience.

"Daddy's going to get me, Jacob. Help me, please."

"I'm right here, Mom. No one is going to hurt you."

"Yes, he is," she hissed and pulled the covers up to her chin. The blackness in her green eyes made the room all the darker. She drew her knees up to her stomach and clenched her teeth. "I can't get away. Keep me safe." She sounded like a six-year-old girl. Jacob's training told him he had to join her hallucinations, not fight them.

"Where are you?" he asked.

"In the house," she said, whimpering.

"And you can hear him coming?"

"Yes," she screamed.

"Okay, he's coming for you. But you have a surprise for him this time," Jacob told her.

"I do?" Rose looked in Jacob's direction without opening her eyes.

"You've let a dog in the house, a big black dog, named Bruce, and you're holding onto his chain. How clearly can you see that?"

"Very clearly," Rose said, relaxing her hands, dropping the sheet. "But Daddy will be mad the dog is in the house."

"Yes, he will, because he doesn't like dogs, does he? And he's going to be scared of that big, black dog named Bruce, isn't he?"

"Yes," she said and laughed like a little girl.

"I want you to tell him you have to take Bruce outside so nobody gets hurt," Jacob kept talking to her like she was a little girl, "because Bruce only listens to you, and your Daddy wouldn't want Bruce to bite him, would he?"

She laughed again. "No, and he's leaving me alone."

"Where are you now?"

"I'm outside playing with Bruce. He's a good doggie."

"That's right," said Jacob. He helped her relax further until she came was able to come back to the present.

Rose took his hand. "Don't ever leave me. You can't abandon me ever, Jacob. I need you."

"Just rest now, Mom. I'm going to call Rue."

"It definitely sounds like a psychotic break, Jacob. That's the best use of Quantum Change I've ever heard of. I'm impressed, love."

"Something must've happened earlier to set it off, right?"

"Indeed. Maybe she'll mention more when she wakes up. You know, Jacob, sometimes when we're given two choices, it appears to us as if we must choose one or the other. But it's nice to know you can choose two things at the same time."

"Sometimes that's true. What are you referring to, Rue?"

"I'm thinking of you going off to college soon. You can practice Quantum Change and be a pastor at the same time. You don't have to eliminate one."

"I know. I just won't have you so close to learn from if I'm in Austin or Ann Arbor."

"There are Quantum Change institutes and trainers in both cities. Axler travels to each of them," said Rue.

"I'll be expected to focus on my major. I'll be learning Latin, German, Greek, Hebrew, all those Old Testament and New Testament courses."

"Expected by whom?" Rue asked.

"Uncle Tommy, mostly, since he's paying for whatever my scholarships don't cover, at least the first year. He said he'll review my grades at Christmas; if he's happy with them, he'll pay for a second year."

"And what will make you happy, love? You don't have to live in Tommy's shadow like your father. Remember, what's been decided can be re-decided."

Rue's words darkened Jacob's thoughts like a shrouded mirror from which sanguinity and longing reflected. In that grieving mirror—the mind of Jacob—floated apparitions and shadows, irrefutable facts, declared by the men of the Murtaugh clan, that optimism prevails, order has dominion over chaos, hard work is the absolute good, and pleasure (or anything exotic which tempts one from natural domesticity) renders the imbecile in pursuit of such foolish notions, maimed for life. For Jacob had already demonstrated his capriciousness when he switched his major from psychology to theology in order to pursue the ministry. To teach him a lesson, the Murtaugh men would make him stick to his choice by controlling the kind of courses he could take in school. Any deviation from his major could cost him their financial support.

"It's more complicated than the control my grandfather, Uncle Tommy, and Uncle Dennis have. My church is sponsoring me as a pastoral candidate; the board of elders promised a scholarship for all four years. The

pastor and vicar wrote recommendation letters for me."
"Seek God, Jacob. But be cautious of His institutions.
Religions of the world are mere ladders meant to bring us
face to face with God—ourselves—telling us to awaken."
Rue lit another cigarette. "What about holidays and
summers? I can mentor you if you come home."
"I probably will come home the first summer. But I
imagine the longer I'm gone, the harder it will be to come
back."
"That seems true of so many things, Jacob."
"I'm suffocating, Rue. Mom is psychotic. Dad is going
crazy. They think I'm schizo. I hate school, but there's
nothing I can do to change any of it."
"You're a boy in a deep hole, love. And you only have a
little time left at home. All you can do is snag a hangnail
on the fabric of reality, and plunge headlong into their
insanity. Otherwise, their craziness will tear you apart,
and you could get lost forever."

Jacob hated mowing the lawn. His only consolation was
his walkman. He drowned out the smoky grind of the
mower (and the world) with Madonna, Debbie Gibson,
and Paula Abdul, pretending he was giving a concert to
hundreds of thousands of fans.

Edwin preferred for Jacob to mow in diagonal lines
to give the yard "contour," but Jacob liked to mow parallel
with the road because it was easier to keep the rows
straight and it made the job easier. He also didn't care to
pick up the piles of rotting grapefruit in the front lawn or
the sticky, decaying branches that had dropped from the

dirty citrus trees.

Let the mower shred them. If the man wants such a manicured lawn, let him come out and do it himself.

Jacob plowed over the fruit corpses and tree limbs like a drunk driver on a rampage. It got the job done, and if he ran over them several times, the blade scattered the evidence thinly enough to disguise it, almost.

While Jacob was performing, *I'll Be There For You* by Bon Jovi, Rose stuck her head out with the portable phone. "Jacob, it's your grandmother." He couldn't hear her so she had to shuffle over in her house shoes and give him a tap when he passed her. Her chin quivered, and the phone shook in her hand.

He turned off the mower and took the phone. Audrey spoke through sobs.

"Baby, I'm so sorry to have to tell you this, but Blake is dead."

The neighborhood was quiet except for the late afternoon zinging of the katydids. A tingling sensation, like bee stings, pricked his neck over and over. His throat tightened as he tried to speak. Images flashed like a slideshow: Blake in a coffin; his bloody body on the road; Blake stabbed to death at home; Blake floating in a creek.

"How, Maw Maw? What happened?"

"He was coming home from night school real late, and his car got run off the road. They think he swerved to miss a motorcycle."

Now Jacob could picture it. Blake in his golden Buick Skylark on a winding, narrow road on a mountain in Cullowhee. A careless driver drifts into Blake's lane. The Skylark goes off the edge and tumbles down the mountain.

"When is the funeral? I want to go."

"It's a closed casket. It was real, real bad, honey. They're burying him tomorrow."

Jacob imagined Blake in the casket. The blue tuxedo he'd worn to his prom fit like clothes on a ventriloquist's doll. There was a white carnation pinned to the lapel.

"Maw Maw, I'm sorry. I have to go." He handed the phone to his mother and ran to his room and lay on the bed, throwing his head on his pillow. He could not hold back the tears, or stop the feeling of being crushed from a pressure on his back that pushed in toward his stomach as if a heavy weight sat on him.

Memories of Blake came to him then: whitewater rafting on the Nantahala; playing battle robots with each other's hands in church; the days and nights they walked up and down the path to the Silver Lining inhaling the scent of Cottonwoods; Orthanach and the Mayor's daughter; the time Blake made him take the driver's seat in that Skylark *while he was driving*; Blake's bony knees resting between his legs in bed talking the night away. Each memory stood in front of another, and as one fell, a different memory stood behind it. The mind sets them up like circles and rows of dominoes with tireless hands, evenly spaced, they run and fall along floor, clicking and collapsing until they take on the shape of a body until one looks with a gasp because each contains a moment (and yet a lifetime) where love was present and is no longer. One chokes at the loss. One staggers at the absurd bargaining and pleading of the mind. One reels at the destruction. The inexhaustible hand places the last domino, and the gasp becomes a howling plea for another, but there are no more.

When Jacob could get off the bed, he rummaged through his desk for every letter, every picture, every memento that Blake had given to him. He put them in a box. He needed a shrine, a place holder until he could make sense of how Blake could be gone.

Blake's face in death, never aging, was always the answer whenever Jacob asked, *What could have been? Where did life go wrong?* As if Blake held some secret knowledge he took with him, and Jacob, having missed his chance to grasp the meaning, remained to journey to other places, and encounter other souls who could show him who he is supposed to be.

The truth Jacob couldn't know, was too hurt to allow for, was this was how love also worked. ❧

CHAPTER XXI

Angels Unawares

Rose straightened her bedsheets and invited Melody and Bryan to sit with her. Better to get the kids talking than to have them keep secrets, she figured. Audrey and Klaus forbade boys in the house. But Rose was progressive. And since Melody had been molested, she had been pushed toward promiscuity; the signs were already there. Rose knew her daughter better than anyone else, she had a mother's instinct; therefore, she would not consult Rue.

"Are you guys having sex yet?" Rose asked. She sat crossed legged in a pink nightie, revealing more leg than Melody was comfortable with.

"Mom, no. I thought we were watching a movie," Melody said.

"Nothing I'd call sex," said Bryan. The words came out of his mouth like gelatin shot through a straw, a wiggling red mess that smeared to the touch.

An orphan at twelve (his mother died of cancer a year

ago; his father abandoned the home long before that), Bryan was working hard on a juvenile record. He and a friend had escaped arrest after a few home burglaries but were nailed when they stole a car and set it on fire. Bryan had promised his friend the insurance payout would be worth it.

Rose felt sorry for him. She could turn him around, she was sure. All he needed was a mother's love.

"It's okay, Melody, kids these days are doing it. I get it. Have you given Bryan a blowjob yet?"

"Oh my God, Mom, that's it. This is gross. And none of your business. Bryan, we're fucking getting out of here."

"Hey, hold on. If my mom was still alive and talked this way, I'd stick around and listen."

"No, Bryan. She's just trying to get attention," said Melody. If there had been a hammer nearby that she could have used to crack open her mother's skull, she would have bashed her between the eyes. But Bryan was excited. The prospect of a fight he could watch, but didn't have to start was better than any movie.

"I am not trying to get attention. And it is too my business," said Rose. "Do you know how many parents would be open-minded like this? Zero. And let me tell you, if your brother knew about you two, he wouldn't like it one bit."

Melody crossed her arms and looked at Bryan. She was trapped. The bitch has a point, she thought. Jacob wouldn't like them dating one bit. He'd never like Bryan and would never understand him. *Jacob is so critical; he wants everything his way, and he thinks he's so perfect* (she often referred to him as The Messiah). Melody held in her heart a half-grudge, for Jacob took more interest in her life than her father. That, she had to give him.

"So what? It's none of his business either," said Melody.

"No, it's not; he won't understand, but I do," Rose said. "I don't want you to let the abuse stop you from enjoying your body. And if you want to talk about sex, I'm here. Sex isn't gross. That's all I'm trying to say. I know men, what they like, I can help you."

"I don't want your fucking help, Mom. Go ahead, Bryan, have your sex talk with my mom. I'm going outside."

Bryan followed her out to the driveway. In the full moon, the sky appeared slate blue. The stars glittered intensely. The whole of it was like a thick blanket pierced with thousands of tiny holes, held up to a brilliant spotlight. Bryan's face was lacquered in gray. "Why do you let her get to you?" He handed her a Newport.

"You try living with the bitch," said Melody.

"She ain't so bad. Could be worse."

"No, she won't just die like your mom. She'll get cancer and then live for twenty years just to make me miserable."

"We aint' got twenty years. You gonna let me sneak in your room when they're all asleep?"

"I don't know, Bryan, probably not. My brother has wonder ears."

"How are we gonna take this to the next level then, Babe?"

"Guess you'll have to settle for blowjobs," she punched his arm and kissed him goodnight.

Frank Teinert was an elder at Messiah Lutheran church. He was short, stout, and worked hard; his life plodded on in regular intervals as faithful as the shadow moves across the sundial. He called Edwin a few weeks after New Year's day and suggested they have breakfast.

"I have a proposition for you," said Frank. He sipped his coffee. He was wearing overalls and rubber boots and an old blue work cap.

Edwin reached for the menu tucked away behind the ketchup and hot sauce. Frank recommended the chicken fried steak with gravy, eggs, and biscuits, as though he were prescribing medication. Edwin ordered scrambled eggs and coffee.

"You're missing out on a real treat, Edwin."

"You've never called me to have breakfast, Frank. Why are we here?"

"Edwin, I'll start with an offer. I need some extra help, and you could use the work. I just picked up a contract to wash an entire fleet of cable trucks. I need to bring in another man. But it's hard on the back, and I doubt you can do it. The offer is there if you want it, but there is something else."

"Talk to Jacob. He'd probably do it. What's the other thing?"

"It's about Rose. This is uncomfortable Edwin, but I was coming home from cleaning some rigs out by Quail Park a few days ago, and I saw her in her car, that maroon Olds with the white top. A man was driving it. They were headed down Hopewell road toward the park."

"In the middle of the day?" Edwin put his fork and knife down and sat back in the wooden seat.

"Before noon. I was suspicious, so I followed them from a distance. They parked under a tree by the big lake."

"What were they doing?"

"They took off their seatbelts, and Rose leaned her seat back. That man's head was bobbing up and down on her for what must've been ten minutes before I realized how bad off I was for looking. I pulled out of there quietly and tried to forget it. But if it had been my wife, I'd want a friend to tell me."

Edwin's mouth was dry. The images stuck in his mind like the overcooked bits of egg clung to his plate. He couldn't bear to insult Frank. He was only the messenger. Should he thank him? Offer to buy his breakfast? Each time he opened his mouth, it was as if he had two tongues. One wanted to keep up a pretense of civility, the other wanted to ask if Frank knew where he could buy a gun.

Sitting in his car, Edwin was surprised by relief. He experienced it as a duality, like a balm that burns and soothes.

He thought he should feel rage like a real man; drive home and yell, and throw things, and demand an explanation. But the more he thought it all through— Rose weeping contritely one minute then clawing at him like a mad cat; the hours (and money) they'd spend "working it out" on Rue's couch; the risk he might have to fess up to his own transgressions—the future suffocated him like black shrink-wrap on a dirty magazine.

He left early from work and took a nap. As he slept, he dreamed the bed was encircled by nine white lights rotating in fiery circles. They made a buzzing noise, each one a different pitch than the other, a harmonic flurry of light. One of them floated above his head.

"I am a seraph. I have been dispatched from the Throne of God to protect you, Edwin."

Edwin reached out his right arm. Suddenly, the white light encircled his head; part of the arc entered his brain. The rest remained out of his head like a halo.

Edwin looked on as the other eight lights returned to Heaven. Catatonic, Edwin's arm remained in the air while the angel spoke.

"I am Reinhardt. The Lord has sent me to guide you. Your wife is committing adultery."

"I'm jealous, but also relieved. Why?"

"Rose is your wife," hummed Reinhardt. "Any husband would feel betrayed. You are relieved because there is a way out," said Reinhardt, as Edwin mouthed the words. "God will grant a divorce both on Earth and in Heaven, and you shall be free."

"Do I confront her?" Edwin asked.

"Not at this time. I will signal you," said Reinhardt.

"What about my job at Rooms To Go?"

"You will keep working there. God has a plan. Your income will not increase so that you will not lose it to Rose," Edwin heard his angel say.

Edwin's arm dropped onto the bed. Peace washed over him. He slept.

"You're not having Bryan over tonight, Melody. I don't feel like company," said Rose.

"You're just going to go to bed, Mom, why do you

care?" Melody picked up the cordless phone in the kitchen to dial Bryan.

"Give me that." Rose grabbed the phone from Melody's hand.

"You bitch. You can call Bruce whenever you want, but I can't call Bryan?"

Like falling cymbals, the noise from Melody stomping outside crashed through the house. Rose slammed the phone onto the receiver and looked out the window. She could only see the orange flare from Melody's cigarette.

"Melody, get back inside," Rose yelled, walking outside. She pinched Melody's arm. "Bruce and I are none of your business."

"Apparently you don't think he's Dad's business either. Let me go or I'll tell."

Rose raised her hand. Jacob walked up from behind her and held her wrist in the air.

"Mom, let her go."

Rose snorted like a racehorse. "I'm going to bruise because of you, Jacob. And I'm going to show your father what you've done to me."

"And I'll tell him what you were going to do to Melody," said Jacob calmly, looking into her eyes and lowering her arm as he breathed with her, letting her relax. "You can't use rage to get her to do what you want, Mom. And I won't let you beat her like you did me."

"I never beat you, Jacob." Rose turned and walked into the house, marshaling excuses like an attorney builds a defense.

"You okay?"

"I hate her," Melody said, leaning into Jacob. "I'm

gonna break her nose the next time we fight, and you might not be here to stop it."

Jacob wondered what was more important to Melody, dating Bryan or getting Edwin to realize there was more going on than just her messing around with a bad boy.

One night, Edwin came home exhausted.

"I'm not hungry," he told Rose.

"I've spent hours in the kitchen, and now you're not going to eat?"

"No, I'm not. I'm going to shower and go to bed."

Melody and Jacob were camped on the couch watching Unsolved Mysteries. Suddenly, Rose screamed from across the house, "Jacob, something is wrong with your father." Jacob ran to their bedroom. Edwin's arm levitated straight above his head.

"Ask your question," Edwin urged repeatedly.

Melody stood in the doorway, giggling. "Somebody should fuckin' ask him something."

"This is Reinhardt, an angel of the Lord. Ask any question."

Such a blessing, thought Rose (who was prone to confiding in psychic hotlines). Jesus had sent a real angel to give her direction. But her Baptist upbringing urged her to test the spirits to see if they were truly from God. "Reinhardt, if you are truly an angel of the Lord, tell me something only I know."

"The one you wish for desires you also."

She was hooked, for it never occurred to her Edwin was "listening."

"This one whose heart I desire," said Rose casually, as if she were requesting an embarrassing item at the pharmacy counter, "Will he leave his wife soon?"

"In time, you will know," said Reinhardt. "Stay on your current path."

"And Edwin? What does Edwin need us to do for him?"

"He needs you to give him time," said Reinhardt.

This encounter began a regular discourse between Rose and Reinhardt. Rose asked him advice about Bruce: when he would leave his wife, how she could help him make that decision, even how to best prepare Edwin for a divorce.

Of course, Edwin let Reinhardt guide her because he had faith that an angel of the Lord had his best interests at heart. ❧

CHAPTER XXII

Absolved From All Allegiance

Jacob had read all he could take on the lonely stretch of interstate outside Pensacola leading into Alabama. There was nothing more to see than a long tunnel of black asphalt with green pine walls flashing by like images in a zoetrope. Inside, he watched the back of his parents' heads bob and sway with the rhythm of the road. He studied his mother's profile as she filed her nails then rubbed cream on her hands hoping it would fade her spreading liver spots. She looked old in the light of the morning sun filtering through the Astro's tinted windows; the deep wrinkles on her face and her set jaw gave her a sinister appearance—she was a woman who had to fight to live, even if she consumed everyone she loved.

Edwin tapped his fingers occasionally on the steering wheel when some old song played on the cassette deck. Otherwise, he stared at the road, past the road, through the horizon, and considered how far a man could go in life. He was forty-six-years old; his eighteen-year-old son was beginning college. Jacob is just starting to live, he thought. I never had a chance to start my life. I could've gone pro, but Tommy had help from all the right people. Business college was hard; Nixon needed more boots on the ground in Vietnam; when we got back, the whole damn country hated us. Nothing like applying for a job when you're getting spit at and the economy was shit. But Jacob will go far.

Edwin would drop Jacob off in Austin, tell his son goodbye, then turn around and go back to his life in Florida. There was a home he still had to pay for, a daughter to protect, a wife to deal with (he would have to put up with Rose a while longer), and work his mediocre job in furniture sales. But at least Jacob was on his way. Jacob wouldn't need him, never really needed him.

Before they left Rich Valley, the family promised they would not fight on this trip to Texas, considering it wouldn't be until Thanksgiving that they would see Jacob again. The past year Melody and Jacob mended their wounds and stopped their quarreling. They never discussed their impending separation, but it was at the forefront of their minds. They had begun camping out in each other's bedrooms on occasion and slept in the same bed sometimes because they fell asleep talking into the night.

Rue warned Jacob to be on watch for Rose and Edwin trying to start arguments because leaving angry would be easier than leaving in grief. Jacob worked hard to stay agreeable and overlook any of their quirks and provocations. Best to have the last memories of family etched with smiles and hugs and promises to phone; not scarred with bitterness and hurt.

What had been so very difficult for Jacob to accept, listening to his mother and father argue about where to stop for lunch, was how deficient they were as parents, as men and women, and as people.

"You think you can find a better place in this town?" Edwin said, turning onto the main road.

"My stomach can't handle the greasy food. But just go. Maybe they have salads." Rose didn't mean it. She was saving another stamp, like the S & H Green stamps grocery stores used to give out. When the book was full, she'd come back to moments like these to collect her reward.

"If you can wait to eat, we can see what's in the next town."

"I told you an hour ago I was hungry. Didn't you hear me?"

They went through the roll call of old sins and unforgivable faults, a familiar account, until Edwin turned the van around and gunned the engine through the light. Lunch would have to wait.

Yes, Jacob had foibles; he didn't consider himself better than everybody else (as Melody often accused him). But he was different. He had tools, and he used them to improve. His mother and father had been offered the same tools, but wouldn't use them. Or they used them to a different effect. His father turned therapy into a crutch to offload his responsibilities. He dug into helplessness like a war trench. Rose twisted Quantum Change and used it to manipulate people.

Jacob looked at Melody. In sleep, her head had fallen to one side and jiggled against the window. A silver strand of drool crawled past her braces down her chin, like a slug's slimy trail. She was going to give them hell. Earning her trust was hard labor—it was a brittle trust— one Edwin and Rose shattered years ago. She was like a purring kitten slinking around your leg. She might let you rub for a bit, but when she's had enough, the claws come out for a scratch and then she's run under the bed to watch until you bring her fish or some milk.

Jacob reclined and tried to focus his mind on college, the dorm, the faceless students carrying books to class. *If you drive looking only in the rear-view mirror, your destination is defined by where you have been.* This was his family's deficiency. At that moment, Jacob understood he was from them, but not of them. Rose and Edwin gave him life, but they were not his life. This was his family, but soon, these people would no longer be his people. He would be a new thing. *But you'll be by yourself,* said The Voice. *What if no one likes you?* An old feeling knocked at his heart.

"But I like me," said Jacob. "And they'll like me too."

"Jacob, what were you dreaming? You were talking in your sleep," said Rose.

"Not really sleeping. Just thinking."

"Don't worry, son. You'll always be my baby boy. Be sweet to people, and they'll be your friend."

When she looked away his disgust amassed into a shape like a mask on his face. "Where's our hotel?" he asked, hoping to shake up the mood.

"We're staying in the middle of the French Quarter,"

said Rose.

"Is there a pool, Dad?" Melody fluffed her matted hair.

Edwin hummed the words to a tune.

"Edwin?" Rose prompted.

"I don't know. These old buildings might not have room for a pool."

"But there is Café Du Monde," said Jacob. "We have to get beignets and coffee in the morning before we head out to Austin."

This wasn't the Murtaugh's first trip to New Orleans. Edwin and Rose made a stop in the city on their honeymoon. They came again when Jacob was three when Tommy was playing in a tournament (at his expense of course). There had been a few other excursions to the Crescent City when Rose needed to get away, but this would be the last time the four of them would ever visit New Orleans together.

After check-in, the family rested at the hotel. There was a pool after all, and Melody and Jacob swam. Edwin and Rose laid out in the sun. They only spoke of practical things: Pass the suntan lotion. How is the air pressure in the tires? How many more miles to go? Have hotel reservations been made for Austin? But nothing about the trip home—without Jacob.

By early evening, everyone was hungry. Rose thought it would be fun to have dinner at a cabaret show. Edwin booked an evening at the swanky club The Cap You Let, where different look-a-like acts such as Liza Minelli, Marylin Monroe, and Barbra Streisand sang their best hits. There was one catch—the performers were all male. The velvet-red curtain closed after Liza. The round spotlight shone on the silver microphone; the stage was set for "Barbara." Jacob looked to his left and then his right, studying the people in the audience who talked past each other mindlessly gorging on overpriced steak and wine. He observed their waitresses; she was over it all, tired of shuffling food to the tables and the empty plates to the dishwasher. Same place, different night; same crowd, new faces. *Are they all looking for real intimacy? Or just a person, an experience to fill the void?*

Streisand began her set with *People*. A few old men clapped as he belted out the words (in sync with the recording). He'd done himself up as late Streisand: he wore a straight, shoulder-length golden wig; a smart white pantsuit with a fake shiny rock on his left hand, and French-manicured nails he fluttered at the audience. His calves were too thick and the earthy gloss on his face, which ended abruptly at the chin line, made him look like he was wearing a rubber Barbara mask. At least he knew he was pretending.

Rose looked at Jacob to catch his reaction. She winked. He smiled and swayed, pretending to enjoy the music to hide his disgust; not at the men prancing on stage in women's clothing, but at the drag his family wore, the drag they made him wear, and for convincing themselves they had passed for the real thing.

Like an ancient iceman being thawed slowly in a lab, something began to yield inside of his body, a release in the muscles, a warming in the chest. Their version of reality that had imprisoned him with encrustations of generational beliefs and fears dissolved as he let go of them, of his past, of their past, of everything he owed them, of what he thought they owed him. Each second felt fresh.

What has been decided can be re-decided.

After breakfast and beignets the next morning, Edwin had it in his mind to get to Austin by late afternoon. This would give them the weekend together before freshman orientation on Monday. He called ahead to make reservations at the Holiday Inn on Town Lake. They had a pool, and it wasn't far from campus.

They pulled into Austin in plenty of time to drive to Lake Travis, grab dinner, and watch the sunset. The restaurant was a jewel hidden on the side of a cliff. Five wooden decks were built in tiers like the terraced rice fields of the Philippines giving each diner a personal, unobstructed view of the lake.

Edwin ordered a beer; Rose drank a margarita; the kids had cokes. When the sun slipped below the silver-blue lake, Austinites and vacationers clapped as if they had witnessed a Broadway performance. Jacob thought of George Washington's wooden chair at the Federal Convention, carved with the half-sun, the one of which Benjamin Franklin said, "I have often looked at that behind the President without being able to tell whether it was rising or setting. But now I know that it is a rising sun." ❧

ISBN: 978-1-54398-553-5

https://akivahersh.com